# DREAD

by Joy Yehle

# Copyright

This is a work of fiction. Names, characters, places, and incidents either are the products of the author's imagination or are used fictitiously. Any resemblance to actual persons, living or dead, businesses, companies, events, or locales is entirely coincidental.

DREAD

Copyright © 2016 Joy Yehle

ISBN-10: 0-9982047-1-4
ISBN-13: 978-0-9982047-1-0

Never Turn Off the Lights
Publishing

## Dedications

For Roy and all the little helpers-
Letitia, Marissa, Trey, Hezekiah, Chloe, Fiona,
and Nayeli.

For my dad, Claude-
Thanks for passing on your love of the
mysterious and supernatural.

For Carmen, my loyal K9 writing partner-
You are missed everyday.

# CHAPTER ONE

From the street, it looked like an ordinary house, but Nate Camden already suspected that things were not exactly as they seemed in Dark Pine Hills. For one thing, because of the name, Pine trees ought to be growing all over the place, but it was as if they had deserted the place along with most of the people.

While it was true that thick towering pines grew in the open space that almost encircled and isolated the subdivision, not a one stood on any residential lot. Instead, the lots contained one of four things: a house, a partial house, weeds, or bare dirt. Not unlike most master-planned communities in the making, except this one had been started years ago and abandoned soon after thanks to the housing mortgage collapse of the early 2000s.

The result was an ugly and unpredictable landscape. An occupied home could be surrounded by empty lots of weeds, or the skeletal remains of a build started but never finished. Sidewalks stopped abruptly and construction debris lay where the workers left it on the last day of paid work. It was as if people had been unexpectedly spirited away by some unseen force.

The development company that Nate's father worked for made some deals and took over the massive project for next to nothing. It was a long-term assignment, and the company gave Nate's family the option of purchasing the original model home for a steal in exchange for him agreeing to take over as Project Manager.

The outside of the house on Canyon Way lived up to its former model home title. A newly installed lush landscaped lawn of Aspens, native flowers, and grass as perfect as a carpet led to two-stories of rock, stucco, and massive sparkling windows. It was like a positive mirror image of the house directly across the street.

Nate glanced at the other house. Windows with no panes gawked jealously at his soon to be lived in house. Weeds crowded the lot, and the porch stairs were missing like a hillbilly resort. Waterproof sheeting across the second floor flapped noisily in the breeze. He watched two crows as big as toddlers hop along the roof. Nate felt a prickle on the back of his neck, and he hoped it would it be one of the first houses his dad's company rehabilitated.

The family huddled on the front porch watching as Nate's dad turned the key and then pushed the heavy oak door open. The first thing Nate noticed was the gleam of the dark wood floor, then the smell hit him. Not the clean scent of new construction or the pungent odor of new paint, but the sickly sweet stench of death.

"Oh my God, David! What is that?" his mom said to his dad, her nose wrinkled.

"Oh, gross!" his sister, Missy, said. She stepped back and pulled her long hair across her face to block her nose.

"You guys stay here. Nate and I will take a look," David said.

Nate's shoulders drooped a little, but he followed his dad inside.

The house was pretty much the way Nate remembered from their initial walk through. The floors and paint were new, the light granite countertops contrasted the dark cabinets, and nothing looked disturbed. David opened the door to the basement, and the stench wafted out. It intensified with each descending step. Nate pinched his nose shut to keep from gagging.

The basement was fully finished and furnished. Large windows allowed sunlight to flood the main room illuminating a pool table and home theater installed to show the model. The features had been left behind, and now they belonged to the Camdens, right down to the fake DVD covers and plastic food on the bar.

They crept along the wall to a short hallway and entered the work-out room. The smell made its way past Nate's pinched fingers. As if on cue, Nate and David looked up at the ceiling to a wet stain growing from the outside wall.

Yep, not a normal house, a sewer or a hiding place for dead bodies or maybe the entrance to hell?

"I think we better call somebody," David said.

Thinking it was some type of sewer leak, David started with a call to the plumber. The man from Big Pipes Plumbing quickly figured out that an exhaust duct ran above the wet spot. An animal, possibly a squirrel, had gotten into the duct from the outside and died while the house stood empty. As soon as the central air conditioner kicked on the bouquet of decay blew throughout the house.

The next call brought a squat man in dusty overalls and a beat up old pickup truck that was more rust than metal. "Wild Animal Removal" was painted on the tailgate in hand-lettering.

"It's a small raccoon. I can't get him out without cutting into the ceiling and opening the duct work. I'm gonna have to get some guys out to replace it. He's pretty juicy. It's gonna probably take a while," the man said, tucking heavy work gloves into his back pocket.

"Well, how long?" Mrs. Camden asked.

"Don't know, he looks like he's been there maybe a week or so."

"Not the raccoon, how long will it take to fix the duct work?" she pronounced every word with force.

"Oh," the man's face flushed. "A few hours depending on when they can get here."

Nate's mom, Mel, pursed her lips together. "We can't move anything in until it's repaired and aired out."

"It's not permanent, but that smell won't be out until maybe tomorrow," the man said.

"Tomorrow? Where are we supposed to sleep?" Missy asked.

"It's fine. We'll stay in a hotel tonight and finish the move tomorrow. Nate can help me move some stuff into the garage for now, and we'll hang around for the repair guys," David said.

"OK, I guess we have no choice. I need help getting some clothes and stuff out of the truck. Maybe the Snow Bird Hotel off the highway?"

"No way. After all this, the four-star Snow Lodge in Morrison," David said.

Missy and Mel happily headed for the twenty-five-minute drive west into the mountains to the hotel, leaving David and Nate to unload some of their belongings from the moving truck into the garage. The three car garage was cleaner than any garage Nate had ever seen. The floors were done in an Indianapolis 500 checkerboard that gleamed in the late afternoon sun.

Nate stuck in his earbuds to block out any possibility that the sounds of a juicy raccoon being pulled out of the duct would reach his ears. That was a sound he felt he would never be able to un-hear.

Poor thing. Nate imagined it struggling, screeching, gnawing trying to free itself until starvation zapped its strength. Did it know death was coming? Did it hurt?

He turned up the volume.

The afternoon heated up considerably. Nate's sweaty arms were itchy against the cardboard of the boxes he moved. He bent to grab the last box. As if to antagonize him, the bottom of the box gave way spilling the contents across the truck bed, down the ramp, and onto the driveway.

Toys.

He should have dumped all that stuff into the donation pile. Ninth grade started in a few days, and he had no need for remote control cars or building blocks, for Pete's sake. He refolded the bottom of the box and began stuffing items back in. Nate discovered his current read under matchbox cars on the driveway.

He checked around for prying parental eyes before he picked up the book and dusted it off. His parents would lay a dozen eggs if they saw what he was reading. His parents were more Hardy Boys, Shakespeare, and college entrance study guide type of approved reading list. A book about Navy SEAL training wasn't going to make the cut. If they knew his reason for reading it, they might even lay a full grown chicken or two.

On one of their many trips to check out the new house before the sale was complete, he noticed a small American flag attached to a sign on Highway 85.

# Navy SEAL
## Danny Dietz
## Memorial Highway

He looked it up on the Internet later and found that Danny Dietz had grown up in the area and served in the Afghanistan War. He was fatally wounded but kept fighting to protect his team until he couldn't fight any longer.

Nate always fantasized about being a big football hero, but this type of heroics was the real deal. The more he learned about the commitment, the determination, the teamwork, all of it, the more it appealed him in his inner most being. If football didn't work out as a career, he set his sights on the SEALs.

He had never had any problem facing any opponent on the grid-iron, it didn't matter if they were older or bigger or stronger. Nate had unwavering confidence in his athleticism, and he felt he had that part of being a SEAL in the bag. The ability to act when life and limb were on the line concerned him. The one time in his life when he had been tested in this area, he had failed.

His family had gone for a day of fishing at a nearby mountain lake. A steady rain had greeted them, and not to be denied a fresh trout meal, the family put on rain gear. Mel pushed through low growing shrubbery to get a better spot at the bottom of the steep bank, but the water made the treads on her rain boots slick. She slipped, and a skeletal tree branch caught her on the way down, jabbing into her outer thigh. When she pulled it out, a surprising amount of blood spurted from the wound.

Nate was right behind her. He saw the whole thing, but he stood there frozen to the spot. Brought by Mel's shout, Missy pushed passed him and dropped next to her. She yanked her jacket off from under her rain poncho and wrapped it around Mel's thigh. David sprinted to them from his spot on the bank and carried Mel to the car. Nate did not move until Missy shouted at him to get in the car.

Mel had been fine. A few stitches and a tetanus shot. Nate had not been fine. Regret and shame filled him anytime he thought about it. Training to be a SEAL would remold that part of him. He was determined to burn out that chicken, coward, wussy part of him.

A car pulled up to the house and a man in a wrinkled suit that resembled elephant hide walked up the front sidewalk.

"Hey, Mike!" David said. He walked to the man and they shook hands.

"How's the move?"

"Not too bad if you don't consider the dead raccoon in the duct," David said motioning to the HVAC truck in the driveway.

"Oh, sorry."

"Ah, the joy of moving," David said.

"I was wondering if you had a few minutes for me to show you some things around the project?"

"My son is here."

"He can come along."

"Yeah, fine. Let me see how much longer the HVAC guy is going to be." David motioned to Nate to come over. "Nate, this is Mike Eubanks, I work with him."

"Good to meet you, sir," Nate and Mike shook hands.

"I've heard lots about you from your dad. You going to play ball down here?"

Nate shook his hand, "Yes, sir. I think so."

"Good, good. The team can use you. Winning teams draw interest for enrollment, which means more house sales," he laughed and cuffed Nate on the shoulder.

"We're gonna go for a quick ride. Can you shut up the garage?" David said to Nate.

"Sure."

They waited for the HVAC guys to finish up and then they loaded up in Mike's car. Nate worried that his sweaty body would stain the expensive dark leather seats.

"Wow, it's hot! Check this out," Mike said with a grin.

Nate felt cool air hit his body where it came into contact with the seat.

"Air-conditioned seats, nice, huh?"

"That's great," David said.

They drove through the wide winding streets. There were several spots where dirt and other construction debris had washed from raw landscapes over the road, making it rough.

"These are the areas we need to concentrate on, unsold and foreclosed lots. Some of the structures were started and abandoned. We will have to demolish them, replace them with our own floor plans. The inspectors will be out sometime next week to advise us on that," Mike said.

David said, "Looks like we may have drainage and grating issues to discuss as well." The tires of the car rumbled over a washout area in agreement.

"We have lots of issues, David. I hope you are up for this. The margins are razor-thin, there's little room for setbacks. I've been on the phone all morning with a nut job from a ridiculous group called the Rocky

Mountain UFO Research something or other. Says we are disrupting a UFO landing area or some inter-dimensional vortex crap. Says they'll join the environmentalists that are actively picketing in the area."

They pulled around a bend to come next to the expansive open space that almost completely encircled the subdivision. The circle was completed by a state park and wildlife area that bordered the homes to the North. Nate knew this was supposed to be the biggest draw with wildlife viewing and plenty of hiking and biking trails.  Their house backed up to the part of the open space called "The Canyons" because of the steep terrain. It was not much for big pines or hiking but made for spectacular views of the Rocky Mountains.

Beautiful as it was, the open space was also the source of controversy. The battle was a familiar one in the west. Keep the land open and wild, or develop it for housing. Environmentalists battled the original developer at every turn. The steady stream of lawsuits had weakened their coffers and when the market nose-dived they couldn't survive.

Nate heard his dad say that the project wasn't handled well from the outset. Construction delays, accidents on the job site, and mismanagement had been their real downfall.

A meager group of people blocked the two hiking entrances from this stretch of road. Some of them were holding signs. He could read one: Human Houses Should Not Destroy Animal Ones.

David groaned.

"Yeah, their baaaaaack," Mike sang.

"They lost in court. Can they legally protest here?" David asked.

"Technically the open space is accessible to the public, so, yes they can. They can't stand around in areas where we are building or residential lots, but they can be here. We agreed to keep public access to the open space to appease these guys. I mean, what more do they want?"

David let out a long breath, "OK. We'll deal with them."

Nate pressed his face to the window with great interest when they drove past the school. Areas of the landscape were still bare dirt and signs of active construction were everywhere. It didn't look like it was going to be ready for students in two days.

Like a beautiful girl with bad teeth, a crack in one of the massive glass entrance doors spoiled the immaculate smoothness of the glass front. The main entry stood two stories high and was faced entirely with glass to take advantage of the western view of the open space and the rugged mountain peaks beyond.

The roof sloped in dramatic angles off to the sides and back. It looked more like a high-tech office building than a school and was at least as big as a hospital. The LED-powered sign out front was emblazoned with "Dark Pine Hills Academy". An animated Grizzly bear loped endlessly across the display.

"There it is! I bet you're not too eager to get in there, huh? Summers are so short now. When I was a kid we got a full three months off," Mike said.

"Yeah," Nate said, but he was very interested to see what it had in store for him.

It was being touted as the model for future schools in Colorado. He wasn't sure what that meant, but he was curious to find out. Nate twisted in his seat to look until the building passed from sight.

"Kindergarten to ninth grade this year. In three years it will be all grades," Mike said. "Nothing else like it in the state."

"I'm glad we got that deal hashed out with the school district. Too bad we had to sell the parcels so cheap to the county, but it makes an excellent selling point. We are an almost totally self-contained community," David said.

"Here's another quaint little feature. Let's stop in here real quick. It was here when the original developer purchased the surrounding land. The owner held out. In the end, it was decided that it would be an asset to the area," Mike said as they swung into the tiny parking lot of a convenience store across the road from the school.

"That's an understatement, considering the nearest grocery store is twenty minutes away in Littleton," David said.

A boy almost as tall as Nate with a mop of dark blond curls that fell across his eyes was working behind the counter. He looked up and smiled when he saw them.

"This is my step-son, Garrett," Mike said.

"Nice to meet you. I'm David Camden, and this is my son, Nate. I think you guys will be in the same grade at the new school together."

"Cool," Garrett said.

The adults moved to the coolers in the back of the store engrossed in a discussion about market value.

"Welcome to Dark Pine Hills. Sounds like an asylum doesn't it?"

Nate chuckled, "Yeah, kinda."

"I'm glad to see humans moving in. It's not like the woods aren't creepy enough, but then everyone bailed."

"Yeah, it is a little weird."

"I've lived here since before the other company flaked out. One day there would be a family in a house and overnight they would disappear. Like something from a horror movie, you know?"

Nate nodded.

"Those freaky protesters think there's some kind of paranormal vortex out in the woods. The construction disturbed it or something. There's a rumor that several guys died when the original building was happening. Somebody fell at the Canyons during building, right off a cliff. Another guy got hit in the dome with a beam or something, killed him instantly."

"I hadn't heard that." A vision of the steep cliffs behind his house popped into Nate's mind.

"Well, hopefully, none of that will be a problem now, right?" Garrett sounded like he was trying to convince himself of something.

"Yeah, for sure. Kind of spooky, though."

"Hmm. Speaking of spooky, school starts in a couple of days, so there's that."

"Yeah, there's that," Nate agreed.

"At least we don't have to ride the bus for twenty minutes to get there now that the new school is open. My mom is happy about that since my little sister is starting kindergarten."

"I have a little sister, too. She's starting seventh grade."

"Cool. Let me give you my number and kickit user, we can hookup, OK?"

"Yeah sure. I don't have my phone on me right now. The charger is lost in the moving stuff."

"Yeah, moving sucks. Maybe you and your sister can come by and use our pool before school gets going," Garrett said as he bent over a pad of pink sticky notes.

"You have a pool?"

"Doesn't everyone?" he grinned a crooked smile and held out his finger with the note stuck to the end.

"Let's go, kiddo," David said as he placed two cans of cold soda on the counter.

Garrett rang them up, and they headed back for home.

Nate was glad to have met someone before the first day of school. Now he wouldn't look like a totally lost loser.

Nate settled into the cool interior of the car and watched the scenery stream past his window. He hoped that Garrett's tale of death and destruction was just a rumor. His thoughts drifted to the raccoon.

Mike stomped on the brake snapping Nate forward against the seatbelt. A woman stood in the road blocking the way. Her face grim, she held a poster board sign in front of her body.

"Get out of the way!" Mike shouted.

She hesitated for moment and Mike laid on the horn. Another protester reached out and grabbed her shoulder, pulling her back to the curb. She held out her sign as they passed. A glittering saucer dominated the poster board. Most of the writing was too small to read, but one word stood out: consequences.

# CHAPTER TWO

The Snow Lodge Hotel would have been better if Nate hadn't had to sleep on the rollaway bed. The room came with two queen beds; his parents took one and Missy the other. The extra bed's mattress was lumpy and flattened to nothing during the night. The pillow was hard as a rock, and a nagging headache had woken him earlier than he liked. But, he made good use of the breakfast buffet in the hotel restaurant, and the headache had lessened quite a bit by the time he polished off his second plate of bacon and hash browns.

His family had headed back to the house on Canyon Way after breakfast. It was way past noon now, and Nate had been moving boxes and furniture with his dad for most of the time. For the last hour or so he worked on unpacking his room. Unfortunately, it looked worse than before the job started. Not only that, but somehow he had reboxed his earphones and had no idea where they could be. He stood staring at the haphazard collection of boxes as if to will the missing earphones to jump out.

A tap on his shoulder broke his attempt to communicate with his quarry.

"What?" he said, turning to see Missy.

"We're going to the dance studio. Mom says you have to come because you're going to check out football."

"Football?"

Missy let out a long-suffering sigh. "Yes. Mom called a guy who says you should come by some park or something and try it out."

"What guy?"

She clicked her tongue and threw her long dark curls behind her shoulder. "Jesus, Nate! Ask Mom yourself. What do I look like? Your secretary?"

"Missy, you don't have to use that tone with your brother," Mel said from the doorway.

"Oh, mom. He's so annoying," she whined.

"Annoying? What did I do? Seriously. You need medication, Missy."

"Nate! That's enough, both of you. Get your stuff. We need to take Missy by the dance studio to register, and the coach of the football team said you should come by their practice today."

"They're already practicing?"

"Well, we missed tryouts. But he says you can still come by today and do a mini tryout, no pads."

"Great."

"It will be fine. Be in the car in two minutes. Missy, you better bring your stuff in case they want to evaluate you, too."

Missy left the room with a toss of her head and a swirling of hair. How was it possible to fit that much drama into such a small girl?

Nate searched for a few seconds to find his football pants and cleats. His mouthguard rattled around in the left shoe. He considered it for a minute. It probably wouldn't be needed for a no-pads-we-already-have-our-starters useless tryout. He stuffed the slightly repulsive thing in the tiny pocket of his pants, just in case.

He thought about something he read in one of his Navy SEAL books, a saying that keeps them motivated. It fit his situation perfectly, *Embrace the Suck*, he told himself.

Against his rights as the oldest, Nate rode in the back seat to the ballet school. Missy complained that his football stuff smelled weird, and if he sat in front, the blowing air conditioner would spread his stink all over her. She could not prepare for her art with that foul stench. Mel gave in to her as usual.

There were times that he felt like strangling his sister. Wrapping her waist-length hair around her neck and pulling. It seemed to him that her only purpose on this Earth was to make his life hell.

"Come in with us. It's too hot to stay out in the car," Mel said to him.

"Can't you just leave the car running?"

"Nate, that's a terrible waste of gas."

He pinched his lips together. He knew there was no point in arguing with her; he hated when she used that voice. It was her insurance investigator tone. It was like truth serum. No wonder his mom was so good at her job.

The temperature was comfortable in the dance studio and a flowery aroma wafted from a plug-in air freshener near the door. The tasteful parent waiting area looked more like a hotel lobby than a dance school. Much classier than the last place Missy had danced. That studio was in the basement of a strip mall and stunk like wet towels that stayed in the swim bag for too long.

Nate sank into the chocolate brown leather couch and searched his cell phone for a good tryout playlist, although he doubted it would matter. Mel and Missy sat across from him in armless side chairs with their heads bent together looking over a schedule.

"Mrs. Camden? This is Sophia Lewis, the dancer I was speaking to you about." A slender woman in a pink leotard and black ballet skirt was standing in front of them. An equally slender girl in a black leotard and skirt stood next to her; they looked like birthday candles on a cake.

"Oh! It's so nice to meet you. This is Missy," Mel said.

The girl gave a quick smile and wave. Missy eyed her.

"Sophia is going to be in ninth grade at your school. Your mother and I thought you could find out about the cheer squad we sponsor through the dance school from her. It's a joint thing between us and the school."

Nate grimaced. This was the first he had heard of Missy being interested in cheerleading, but it would be a good fit for her big mouth. He almost laughed out loud but turned it into a cough. The ladies turned and glared at him.

"Excuse me," he mumbled and hunkered back to his phone.

"I'm not a captain or anything, right now it's just mostly girls from the dance studio. But there's tryouts for anyone who wants to join next week at the school. JV and level III. I'm JV." Sophia said.

"OK," Missy said.

"I can help you learn the cheers ahead of time if you like."

"Really?"

Sophia shrugged, "Sure. Can you stay for a while today? We pretty much have the rehearsal studio all to ourselves."

They left Missy to rehearse with Sophia and headed back to the new school. The two girls were giggling together as if they had known each other for years. Two minutes before Missy had eyeballed the other girl as if she were a poisonous spider. The secret behavior of girls was mystifying. Nate was more than ready to be around some guys.

Nate hadn't been able to see the playing field yesterday because it was tucked into a lower area at the back of the school. It didn't become visible until he and Mel walked around the building. Nate was surprised to discover the field was artificial turf and even more surprised when the man that greeted them told Mel it was heated to melt snow.

"We're looking for Coach Summer?" Mel asked.

"No, not me. That's him down there. Hey, Coach!" the man called.

A man on the sidelines with a clipboard turned their way. His sweat-wicking shirt clung to a physique that looked much younger than his hairline. He marched up to Mel and Nate as if on a mission.

"Mrs. Camden," he said. "I'm Coach Summer. This must be Nate."

"Nice to meet you," Mel said.

"Good to meet you, sir."

He considered Nate the way a person at the meat counter looks over the cuts of steak.

"You're tall and filled out for a ninth grader. Is your dad tall?"

"He's close to 6'2", I think."

"You been working out over the summer?"

"I run and lift almost every day."

"Your mom says you play wide receiver."

"Since I was nine, sir, but I can play any position. Even quarterback."

Coach Summer snickered, "I think we're all set there, but let's see what you got."

Mel moved to the bleachers and Nate warmed up. He noticed the other boys on the field had stopped practice and were checking him out. His pulse picked up. He tried to concentrate on his breathing and to clear his mind of all the thoughts that were speeding through.

Making this team, even if he wasn't a starter, was the most important thing in his life for the next fifteen minutes. He would make the most of it. Nate had done his best to envision the field and the things he would be asked to do in the car ride from the dance school. Another thing he had learned from the SEALs.

Now feeling the familiar crunch of turf under his cleats, his mind became calm, his breathing controlled, and the world around him melted away. He was relieved to slip into his zone so easily. Although he'd been doing it for most of his life, he wasn't sure how it would be on a new field with new teammates.

His mom's voice popped into his head for just a second, it's just a game, not real life. Right at this moment, he knew that wasn't true. That was something parents said when they didn't fully support what you were doing, but he knew this was his calling even if she didn't.

The coach had him run sprints, a few agility moves and threw a few balls to him. He called the other coach over, and the rest of the boys stood by. Coach Summer showed him the clipboard where he had been making notes. The second coach let out a low whistle.

"Let's run 'em in traffic," Coach Summer said.

Nate took his position on the field with some other players. Since they were practicing without pads, there were four guys lined up on the defensive side.

"Nate run the route I just had you do. Bryce, that's 22!"

An athletic blond-haired boy in the quarterback position waved acknowledgment to the coach and smiled a toothpaste commercial perfect grin.

"You ready?" he asked Nate.

Nate nodded.

A boy on the defender side shouted at Nate, "There's a fee for late sign ups, kid. Let me show you the bill!"

The other boys laughed. Nate cracked the knuckles on his right hand and wiped both hands on his pants.

Bryce called the snap. Nate ran the route, muscle memory compelling his body to move and angle the right way. His cleats dug into the turf, leaving the trash-talking kid in his ready stance. The ball landed in Nate's arms like a bird returning to her nest. He looked to the coach.

"Holy crap, kid! Are you fast!" Bryce shouted.

Nate heard sounds of approval from the other boys. Coach motioned for Nate to come to the sideline and Mel joined them.

"You're good, Nate. Really good. I wouldn't be able to start you. These other boys have been practicing for three weeks already, and I need a sports physical sign-off, and you have to have an official weigh-in. But I'd love to have you."

"I'd love to be here."

"Fine! Great! Mrs. Camden, I'll email you all the forms we need filled out. We practice Tuesday to Friday unless we have a Friday game. Games are on Fridays or Saturdays, usually," he rambled. "We're only JV because we have no seniors, yet. But we're building a first-class program. College scouts are already wanting to come by."

"Hey kid, pass me the ball!" a boy shouted to Nate.

He didn't realize he was still clutching it. Nate threw an easy pass to the kid. The ball bounced out of his hands and continued to roll across the field and bounce into the woods beyond. The kid looked back at Nate, eyes wide.

"Go get it, Eric!" Bryce shouted at him.

Eric shook his head. "You go get it!" he shouted to another boy.

"No way, man!"

"Oh, for crying out loud!" Coach Summer pulled another football out of a large duffle bag and tossed it to them. "I've never seen a bigger bunch of babies!"

"What's that about?" Mel asked.

"Oh, you know kids. Ghost stories about the woods." He shook his head.

Nate was about to ask what ghost stories when a terrible wail from the field drew their attention.

A boy was flat on his back holding his knee to his chest and howling. The assistant coach and some other players trotted his way.

"Well, a starting position may have just opened up. Good luck for you," Coach Summer said.

"Yeah, good luck," Nate said.

The tears and pained look on the other boy's face didn't look much like luck.

# CHAPTER THREE

Nate double-checked his phone for the address Garrett had given him. The house was in the custom homes part of the development, in an area called "The Backcountry." Here, the homes were big, and the lots were bigger. The house he pulled his bike up in front of was an impressive spread of stone and timber. The lawn was perfectly groomed and landscaped to look like a mountain meadow.

Garrett said to go through the side gate and around to the basement entrance. The backyard was even more impressive than the front. The stone of the house swept down into an impressive outdoor fireplace and kitchen. Beyond that, a stone walkway led to a swimming pool and built-in hot tub. Music seeped out of a set of French doors.

Nate knocked hard.

The doors opened, and the music crashed out. Grinning, Garrett held the door open for Nate to come in.

"Hey! Turn it down!" he shouted.

The basement wasn't what Nate had pictured, either. The stonework from outside repeated inside to build a wet bar and fireplace. An expensive-looking pool table dominated the area. He could see beyond that through a cracked doorway to a home theater that made his look like a discount store special.

"Wow, nice place," Nate said.

Garrett smirked. "Thanks. My parents are freaks."

He gestured for Nate to sit down on the leather couch that faced the fireplace. The massive mantel was stuffed with trophies. Garrett's name was engraved under the snowboarding figurines and pillars.

"You snowboard?"

Garrett looked sheepish. "A little."

"Looks like more than a little."

Garrett shrugged. "I wiped big time last season and got a bad concussion." He moved his hair off his forehead, an angry red scar started above his right eye and disappeared into his hair. "My mom's a doctor, so she's making me take time off. She's worried that I'll get brain damage. Too bad for my brain, I'm trying to learn to skateboard."

A girl with short jet-black hair popped up from behind the bar. She had on peacock blue glasses that matched the streaks in her hair. The light glinted off a tiny diamond stud in her nostril.

"Is that better?" she asked, gesturing with a remote, the music volume noticeably lower.

"Yeah. Nate, this is Lindsey Pyre. She lives up the road."

"Hey," she said.

"Hey."

"Are we gonna swim or what? Nate, there's a bathroom right there if you want to change," Garrett said pointing across the room.

It wasn't so much a bathroom as a spa. The room contained the usual bathroom items but sported a steam shower big enough for two people. Nate felt awkward changing in the upscale space and didn't want to mess anything up. By the time he finished, Garrett and Lindsey were already in the pool.

He threw his towel over one of the lounge chairs and waded into the water. A small body with a mass of curly hair sprang past him; he sucked his breath in as the cold water splashed his head and chest. A smiling face with eyes the same shade of green as Garrett's popped up from beneath the water.

"Haley!" Garrett shouted.

"I wanna swim too!" She pushed wild strands of hair from her face. "You have big muscles," she said to Nate.

He felt his face go hot.

"Mom! Get Haley!"

She spun in the water and kicked away from Nate. "Lindsey, can't I swim with you guys?"

"Only if we play Mr. Shark, and I get to be the shark!" Lindsey dove under swimming fast toward Haley.

Haley squealed and headed directly for Nate. She grabbed him around the waist, giggling.

"Mom! Sorry, Nate. Little sisters," Garrett said.

"It's fine. Come on, Haley, let's get outta here. Hang onto my neck." Nate dove away from Lindsey. He went far enough under to keep Haley on the surface and pulled hard with his arms. When he surfaced, Haley was laughing, and they were now almost to the opposite side of the pool. Nate had been careful not to go too deep or too far away from the side. It wasn't that he didn't know how to swim, but he knew his limitations. The water was another hurdle to his goal of the SEALs.

"Hey! No fair!" Lindsey called. The sun glinted off the surface of the pool and made the water beads on her skin sparkle like her diamond nose stud.

She wore a one-piece blue and gray swimsuit that hugged her curves in a way Nate couldn't help but notice.

"Cannonball!" Garrett, hugging his knees to his chest, hurled himself into the pool covering them all in a wave of turquoise water.

Haley sputtered and choked. Nate pulled her off his back to get a look at her. She moved her mouth like a fish out of water. Nate froze. Anxiety making his lungs seize up along with Haley's. Much to his relief, Garrett grabbed her.

She let a long hacking cough. "Garrett, you big dummy!"

Garrett's mom didn't respond to him calling her, but like most mother's her hearing was especially acute to the youngest. She magically appeared at the side of the pool.

"Come on baby, let the big kids swim alone." She held her arms out to Garrett and Haley. "I'm Garrett's mom, Jen. You must be Nate."

"Yeah, nice to meet you."

Garrett lifted Haley to the side of the pool. Jen wrapped her in a big fluffy beach towel, her tiny pink feet sticking out at the bottom. "Garrett, you need to be a little more careful when Haley is in the pool."

"Sorry, Haley."

She waddled into the house with her mom without a word or glance back at them.

Lindsey scooped a palm full of water into Garrett's face. "Yeah, Garrett. That's for Haley." She threw her head back and laughed.

Garrett shook his head and looked to Nate. "Women."

They spent the rest of the afternoon splashing each other and playing keep-away with a small football. It was fun, but Nate couldn't shake the stone of shame and disappointment that had formed in his gut. What if Haley had really needed help? He had just stood there like an idiot. No, worse, like a coward.

Lindsey and Nate decided to leave right around the same time. Lindsey was changing in the bathroom that Nate had used earlier. Even though it was early evening, it was still hot, and Nate opted to ride home in his damp swim trunks. He put on his shirt, socks, and shoes, and shoved the rest of his stuff in his backpack.

He rode at a leisurely pace and took some time to take in the neighborhood. For the most part, he streamed past empty lots full of abandoned construction debris. Thick pines of the open space were visible from the flat, empty spaces. The air filled with their clean and soothing scent. In places, the trees stood so close together that only a paper-thin person or small child could fit between them. Every little while a complete home with a newly sodded yard would pop up like a butte rising from the desert floor. His dad's company was making progress.

He rode past the newly-finished skate park. Every skate park he had ever seen was always crawling with kids, even when school was in session. This one was completely deserted. It was getting dark, but the lights had come on, and the ramps were well lit. Nate guessed that maybe there weren't very many skaters in his new neighborhood.

He pulled up to his house, entered the garage door code, and put his bike away.

The house was quiet and cool when he walked in. He'd be on his own for dinner. David was working late, Mel had a late meeting, and Missy was at ballet class. He pulled the refrigerator open and stared at the boring contents. His taste buds could go for some pizza and a coke, but all he found was baked chicken breast and quinoa leftovers. His mom would not serve them pizza if her life depended on it and soda of all kinds was strictly forbidden. He comforted himself knowing that the healthier fare was better for him and supported his goals better than empty calories ever could. But chugging a coke right now would have been great.

He trudged upstairs, peeled off his damp trunks and got in the shower. The hot water prickled his cold skin, and he let it run over him until he drained the water heater. If his parents had been home, he would have kept his shower to an earth-friendly six minutes. But they weren't and he didn't.

He put on basketball shorts and a Colorado Avalanche t-shirt and padded barefoot downstairs. He shoved a plate of chicken leftovers into the microwave and let his thoughts wander. They didn't go very far before they came back to Lindsey.

When they were playing catch, she held her pointer finger up to signal she was number one. There was a brightly-colored peacock feather tattooed down the inside of the finger. He envisioned a few places on her body where other secret artwork might be. The microwave dinged, pulling his thoughts back to the kitchen.

He thought he heard a light knock on the front door as he dropped the hot plate with a clang onto the counter top. It must be Missy. She always forgot her keys.

Nate pulled the door open and was surprised to see two boys standing there. One about his height and age and the other much younger. Nate noticed that their hair was the same shade of blond and the thought passed through his mind they must be brothers. In fact, they looked exactly alike, like twins, only that couldn't be right.

"Hello, we were heading for the market when we realized we forgot our money. We were hoping you would be kind enough to let us in to use your phone," the older boy said.

Nate's brain felt foggy, like after a hard hit in football. "You have to call for the money? The market?"

"Yes, yes! We have to phone for someone to bring us the money!" he said with a smile.

The kid's teeth were so white they almost glowed. There was something artificial about the smile; it reminded Nate of dentures. He glanced at the younger boy, and he was smiling and nodding in agreement. Nate felt himself open the door a little wider.

"Yes, we need to come in," the younger boy said in a voice that seemed much too high and sweet for him, like the voice of a tiny girl.

Nate's breathing slowed down. His limbs felt heavy like they did when he was drifting off to sleep. He willed his eyes to look the boys over again. They seemed harmless, and all they needed was the phone. He tensed his body to step aside and let them in. The taller kid's eyes flashed something that did not fully register with Nate's brain. He recoiled inwardly like seeing a dead animal on the side of the road.

A car pulled into the driveway and momentarily blinded him with the headlights. Nate held up his hand to shield his eyes and in that split second, the boys vanished. His brain immediately came out the fog, and he focused to see his little sister being walked to the door by Sophia.

"Hi...my Dad...we drove your sister home." She quickly looked away from him as Missy pushed past, almost knocking him over.

He realized he was staring with his mouth hanging open. He snapped his mouth shut and swallowed the stale saliva that had pooled under his tongue.

"Thanks, Sophia. I'll see you at school tomorrow," Missy called around him.

"Sounds good," Sophia said. She waved and got in the car.

Nate stepped to the end of the porch and surveyed the yard. Where had those kids gone? He scanned the bushes, nothing. Up and down the street, still nothing. The weeded yard of the empty shell of the house across the street stood undisturbed. He rubbed his eyes with both hands. Was he sleepwalking or something?

"Hey, close the door, you're letting in bugs!" Missy said.

He turned and looked at his sister. She was scowling at him.

"What?"

She raised her eyebrows and put her hands on her hips. She looked like a younger version of their mom.

He didn't know what to say. "Sssso you're friends with Sophia?" It was lame, but it was the best he could do.

"Oh my God, really? You are such a boy. Yes, we take dance together, and we are friends. Like you didn't know that. Why? As if I didn't know based on your drooling."

"I'm not!"

"Yes. You are. Sophia's on the squad for cheer at school, and she has been helping me get ready for tryouts."

"Oh."

"Oh? That's all you have to say? God, you are such a dork." Missy flipped her hair over her shoulder, kicked her dance bag aside, and trotted toward the kitchen.

"Did you see anyone on the porch?" he called after her.

"What do you mean? Besides my hormone-crazed brother?"

"Shut up! No, there were some kids out there right before you guys pulled up."

"I didn't see anyone but you, unfortunately," she called from the kitchen.

"Whatever," he mumbled. Maybe he had hit his head in Garrett's pool and didn't realize it. Maybe he had a brain injury from football that was just now showing. Maybe he wasn't crazy, just injured. Neither alternative was a good one.

# CHAPTER FOUR

A clamor of raven's caws warned her when she opened the car door.

She always hated ravens and believed wholeheartedly that there was a good reason that a flock of them was called an unkindness. Childhood stories taught her that they were messengers of bad news, but she would not accept that on such a glorious morning. Everything was fresh and clean, right down to the air.

The early news report said that a storm was expected later in the day, and she knew how fast the weather could change, but it didn't look likely judging by the clear blue sky above her.

But isn't that how it happened? It might have been a cliché, but it was true. Everything plugging along one second and then a phone call comes, or a door opens, and then nothing is ever the same. She pushed the thought away and opened the trunk of her car.

She gathered her teaching bag, purse, and a box of the final touches for her classroom. Usually, not much went up on the walls. Instead she let the students decide or create what went there. Her desktop, however, was her domain. Moving a few things aside, she double-checked to see that her favorite coffee mug survived the move. The box had been packed away for over a year. That was the last time she had been in the classroom.

She needed to get back to work as a positive step in her grieving process and returning to a normal life, whatever that meant. The last year had been spent working up to this, and each step to the entrance was a like a mini-declaration of her intention to be whole.

She stepped over unopened boxes of tiles meant to cover the bare floor just inside the entrance. The sounds of construction came from everywhere and by the smell of it, the painting was still ongoing. She hoped the building would be ready in time. It's cutting-edge green construction and unprecedented technology was being flouted by the school district as a model for all future schools in Colorado. A postponement in the opening would be a political disaster for the new school board members. Opponents would pounce on the chance to point out the waste of taxpayer dollars.

She climbed the massive stairway just off the main entrance to the second floor. The lights were off down the corridor, but her classroom door was just outside of the natural light coming in through the massive wall of windows in the entry.

The school layout consisted of one main building that housed the high school and two wings. One for the elementary and one for the middle school. She'd never been at a school that housed kindergarten to twelfth grade on the same campus. The design was based on research that found this configuration supported community and collaboration between age groups. Which in turn was supposed to translate into well-rounded higher-achieving students. Critics were already predicting a less favorable outcome, but she was hopeful.

She smiled when she approached the door and saw her nameplate affixed to the space next to the door in bold black letters, Ms. Linda Garza. It wasn't the first time she had seen her name in print since she began using her maiden name again, but it seemed important to see it here, in this place.

Her classroom was dimly lit and the sounds of the building muffled by the door. She unpacked her box placing each item just so on her desk. She didn't need to report officially for about an hour, but she wanted some alone time in her new space.

The sound of the door to the classroom next to hers clicking open signaled the arrival of her neighbor. She met Inna Kerpin for the first time yesterday at the initial staff meeting, but they hit it off right away. They both found the humor in a Canadian with a Russian name teaching American History and a woman whose first language was not English teaching English Language Arts.

She left what she was doing to pop over and say hi. Above everything else, it felt good to have a friend again.

The corridor was dark. She heard a door bang shut somewhere down in the darkness. She pulled on the door handle to Inna's classroom and found the door locked. Linda peered intently through the small side window into the blackened room, straining to see anything. She jumped when a hand touched her shoulder.

"Oh! Sorry!" Inna said.

Linda laughed. "Oh my God, you scared me! I thought I heard you go in a minute ago."

"Nope, I just got here. Here, hold these," Inna said, and she shoved a white bakery bag at Linda. "Donuts, the breakfast of champions."

"They smell good."

"I brought one for you," Inna said.

Inna pushed her key into the door lock and instead of the quiet clicking of tumblers falling there was a loud bang that was felt as much as heard. They stared at each other with wide eyes and hearts thumping. It took a second or two for it to register it had to be noise associated with the construction.

They both burst out in laughter.

At that same moment, on the other side of the building and one floor below, the cheer team was finishing up an early morning workout. Some of the girls screamed and ducked down as the exposed duct work in the locker room reverberated from the percussion.

A girl with blonde hair so luminous it glowed in the low light of the locker room peeked over the bench she and several girls hunched under. Her green eyes narrowed when she saw the open water bottle resting on the bench.

"Calm down, it's just construction!" the coach said.

The blonde quickly, impulsively, reached out and knocked the water bottle over just as the other girls stood up.

Nervous laughter and chicken sounds filled the room.

Sophia didn't get a chance to laugh. Her open water bottle must have got knocked off the bench when they took cover, and the contents had emptied right into her bag. She carried the dripping mess to the sink and tipped it over. A surprising amount of water poured out.

"Oh, like that really sucks," the green-eyed beauty said.

"Tell me about it."

"I'll wait for you."

"Really? Thanks, Kim."

Sophia dried her stuff out the best she could with the hand drier. After several minutes, everything was still wet, but she stuffed it back in the damp bag. It took so long that everyone else bailed, including Kim, leaving her alone in the locker room.

So much for changing into normal non-sweaty clothes and having someone to walk out with. She looked down at herself. Water had dripped on her shoes making them soggy. Her shorts were too short and her tank top too tight for anything but working out. But, she would have to walk home in them. Awkward. It was still early in the day; no one would see her. Hopefully.

She tugged her shorts down and tried to stretch her shirt out with little success. If this was any sign of how the ninth grade was going to go, it was going to be a long year. She yanked her tank top up by the straps in frustration, causing her to wince.

Pulling up the bottom of the shirt she studied the angry, red, scabbed over slices in the delicate skin under her breasts. Sophia fingered the gashes gingerly and felt glad that the hard workout had not opened them. Bleeding through her shirt would have been hard to explain. The bottom of her sports bra rubbed painfully against the cuts, but it was the only place she could cut and hide it. Any lower and her cheer uniform would give her away. Her arms and legs were usually bare for dance and cheer, so it really was the only place.

You can just stop. That was the lie she repeated to herself.

Letting her top fall back into place, she took a deep breath, threw her head back, and took fourth position. Right foot behind the left, the toes of her right foot tucked into the heel of her out-turned left foot. Left arm up, right arm gracefully turned in at the elbow. She did a slow relevé to her tippy-toes, aware of the tautness of her body.

Sophia startled when she heard the door to the locker room jiggle. She spun to face the door, a wash of embarrassment flushed her face with heat as if she had been caught picking her nose. The door remained shut and still. Her breath let out in a slow stream. Taking her stuff off the counter, she half-jogged for the door.

She had to go through the gym to get out of the building. A sliver of light from the small windows in the doors that led to the corridor beyond tried to jab into the darkness only to be strangled by the gloom. Her wet shoes protested against the gleaming hardwoods with a shriek.

She glanced around and thought for a second she saw movement in the shadows of the far corner. She froze.

"Hello?"

Silence.

Squinting into the darkness, shadows began taking familiar shapes of bleachers and tumbling mats. Sophia shook her head, annoyed at her silly behavior. But she walked a little faster and was grateful to step out into the light of the corridor.

Rather than walk all the way to the main doors she headed for an exit door at the end of the corridor. The shortcut would save her from having to walk all the way around the building to head home. Through the slim window at the side of the door, she saw a boy standing there. He waved to her. She could see he was dressed oddly for late summer, jeans, and a long-sleeved flannel shirt.

"Hey miss, can you please open the door for me?" The door muffled his voice.

*Miss? Why did this kid talk so weird?* All the hairs on the back of her neck stood at attention. Adrenaline flooded her muscles.

*What the heck? It's just some kid.* She inched closer to the door.

"Please let me in," he said.

She hesitated. Something felt off. She couldn't get a good look at him, but he seemed normal enough, just dressed weird.

*Maybe he was homeless. In this area? Not likely.*

*Maybe he was one of the protesters and needed to use the bathroom.*

*Maybe he was a protester and wanted in to vandalize the new building to make a point.*

*Maybe he was a crazed kid serial killer, and a girl all alone in a school was a good victim.*

Her muscles weren't going to wait for her brain to answer.

"I can't."

She spun on her heel and walked as fast as she could in the other direction. She could hear the kid, yelling now. Hollering that she needed to let him in. The anger in his voice validated her instincts. She picked up her pace to a full-out sprint.

Sophia burst through the main doors never slowing and not looking back. It was irrational, but she knew if she looked back he would be right behind her. A storm had blown in, and the wind pushed against her, slowing her down.

Her lungs didn't burn until she reached her front porch. Panicking when she realized her house keys sat in the bottom of the soggy mess of a gym bag, she let out a frustrated squeal. Tipping the entire bag upside down she shook hard, and everything clattered onto the porch. Her keys were buried under clothes sticky with water. She clutched at the keys, scraping her knuckles on the hard surface of the porch. Her hands were shaking so badly it took longer to get the key in the lock than it should have.

Shoving the door open she fell inside and slammed it shut. She tripped on the small welcome rug in front of the door and fell to her knees. Sophia flipped over onto her rear end, and stared wide-eyed at the door, waiting for the handle to jiggle or a face to peer in through the little window at the top. Several seconds passed, but it felt like hours to her.

The handle remained still, the window empty.

Her breathing slowed down, and the adrenaline drained from her system, releasing her brain to more rational thought.

What was that about? That kid hadn't tried to hurt her or follow her. He yelled at her, but he was just pissed that she wouldn't let him in.

She put her hand to her ribcage and pressed her fingers into the soreness there, releasing more relief. She felt like she had run a marathon instead of the two or three miles to her house.

Anxiety attack. That had to be it. She had them often enough to know that was likely what had happened. But still, this one had been different. Usually, it was a tightening in her chest, a racing heart, muffled thoughts, and then the paralyzing sense that death was coming. Today it was full flight or fight. Maybe her anxiety was getting better. Or worse.

Her stuff on the porch would have to wait. For now, she needed her familiar ritual to release the anxiety.

# CHAPTER FIVE

That night, Nate dreamt of wandering, hopelessly lost in a maze of hallways and doors that would not open for him. He woke up several times during the night but returned to the dream every time. Thankfully, the dream was not prophetic and his first morning at the new school had been uneventful.

It helped that all the ninth grade classrooms were on the second level in building one. He glanced away from his algebra to the clock, ten more minutes. His stomach growled now, but he would have to tough it out.

He realized that he had no one to eat with at lunch. At his old school, he and his friends had sat in the far corner of the cafeteria. The table they sat at had a wobbly bench, and no one else wanted to sit there. That bench had been the source of many gut-busting lunch periods and a few table-wiping detentions. He looked around for a familiar face. Nobody. He'd figure it out when he got there.

He jumped a little when his phone vibrated in his front pocket. That was one thing he had to get used to. At this school he wasn't just allowed to have his phone in class, it was encouraged. Teachers sent pictures, videos, reading assignments, and other class materials to a website accessible from a smart device app. His American History teacher had sent pdf files of maps during class so they could look at them and use them later for a homework assignment. She had even encouraged them to text questions to her during class.

He slipped the phone out and peeked at the screen.

*Garrett: See you at lunch*
*Nate: Cool*
Problem solved.

At lunchtime, he entered the cafeteria to find what looked like loosely-controlled chaos. He searched the heads for the familiar mop of curls. Somebody slapped his lunch sack out of his hands from behind.

"Where you going, rookie?" It was a guy from the football team. Nate wasn't sure of his name, but his number was 22.

Nate shrugged and snatched up his brown paper bag.

Bryce stepped through the crowd, "Come on, Nate. Let's eat!" He put his arm around his shoulders in a partial headlock and led him away.

They stopped at a table in the middle of the room. There were kids already sitting there. They had their heads bent together as one of them played a video game on his phone. Nate pulled his head out from under Bryce's arm to look for any openings and in the hope he would spot Garrett.

"Get lost, losers. This is our table," 22 said.

"Hey guys, let's find a different table," Nate said. But when he looked down the gamer kids had gathered their stuff and vanished.

Nate sat down with the rest of them. He pulled out his phone and texted Garrett.

*Nate: where are you*
*No reply.*

Some of the boys wandered off to get in the line to buy lunch, leaving Nate with a few of the others. He recognized one boy as the player that had gotten hurt, the boy whose place he would be taking.

"How's the knee?" he asked.

"It's not too serious. Just my ACL."

"Can you play?"

"Nah, need surgery, but it has to wait."

"Too much swelling?"

The kid shook his head and shrugged.

"Cooper's dad got laid-off. No insurance," Bryce answered.

"Oh man, I'm sorry."

"It's cool. I'll be back next year."

"Oh, sure, yeah," Nate said.

The lunch buyers returned to the table with a clatter of plastic trays and rough-housing. Nate was grateful for the distraction, but guilt had surpassed his appetite. He threw most of his lunch in the garbage.

He didn't hear from Garrett until he was entering his English Language Arts class, the last of the day. Entering the classroom, he spotted Garrett sitting at a table under the window. As soon as he saw Nate, he smiled and motioned him over to an empty seat.

"Sorry about lunch, man."

"Nah, it's cool. What happened to you?"

"I had to meet with the principal."

"Wow, first day and you are already in the principal's office?"

"No, not like that! It's kind of embarrassing."

"Oh, now I gotta know," Nate said.

Garrett shrugged. "I have freakishly mad math skills, and I might have to take my math class on the internet instead of in class."

"For real?"

"For real."

"That's cool! Dude, I wish I had any kind of math skills."

Garrett smirked, "Not too nerdy for you?"

"Hell no! Now I know who to copy off of."

More kids poured in and filled in the empty chairs. Nate saw Sophia come in and slink to the back of the room by herself. She was wearing a cheer uniform, and her hair was tied up in a neat ponytail that fell to the middle of her back. She looked perfectly put together but moved with a stiffness of someone who was ill.

The bell rang, and a tiny bronze-skinned lady with short dark hair walked to the front of the class.

"Good afternoon, students," she said. "I'm Ms. Garza. We will do a lot of reading, writing, and discussing in this class. All I ask is that you respect your fellow learners and myself, and we will be fine. I know you all hate this, but we are going to go around the room, state your name, and tell us one interesting thing about yourself or your favorite food. I'll start. Like I said, I'm Linda Garza and the interesting thing about me is I speak Spanish fluently, if you couldn't tell from my little accent. My family is from Guatemala, but I have lived here since I was about ten years old. Next."

She was right; Nate hated this. He struggled to think of something interesting. As it got closer to his turn, he thought he might open his mouth and nothing would come out. He could tell them that the most interesting thing about him was his dad was white and his mom was black, but that seemed weird. It was obvious that his family tree was more diverse than any of theirs.

"I'm Kimberli Price, that's Kimberli with like two i's. The interesting thing about me is that I love to cheer, if you couldn't tell," a girl sitting across from Nate said. She had on the same uniform and similar hair style as Sophia, but her makeup was much more dramatic. Bright-blonde corkscrew curls stuck out at her temples like the curling ribbon on an overdone balloon bouquet. She set her green eyes on Nate and flashed a toothy grin.

"Um, I'm Nate Camden and, um, my favorite food is pizza."

"I'm Garrett Moss and my favorite food is pizza." He and Nate high-fived.

Ms. Garza laughed. "Isn't that interesting. And last but not least."

"I'm, um, Sophia Lewis. The, um, interesting thing about me is that I, um, love ballet."

"I love ballet too, Sophia! I have seen the Nutcracker every Christmas, well, almost every Christmas. Do you dance?"

Sophia's face flushed, and she nodded.

"Excellent!"

Nate watched Kimberli turn her back to Sophia and roll her eyes. He looked at Garrett, but Garrett was staring open-mouthed at Sophia. Nate nudged him under the table. Garrett snapped his mouth shut and gave Nate a crooked grin.

"Our first unit is a short one, an easy way for us to ease back into school." The room rustled with approval, and Ms. Garza held up her hand for silence. "It's called Around the Campfire. Based on that title, what do you think it will be about?"

"Smores!" someone shouted.

Ms. Garza laughed, again. "Not exactly."

"Stories told around a campfire?" Garrett offered.

"Bingo! It's a bit more than that, really. We are going to look at tall tales, urban legends, and cyberlore. What are they? Why are they told? How they apply to our lives."

"Some urban legends are true, aren't they?" a voice from the front of the room asked.

"That's what we will find out. Who knows an urban legend they are willing to share?"

Kimberli raised her hand; Ms. Garza nodded at her.

"Well, this one really happened to a girl my old boyfriend knows." The room giggled. "No really," she glared.

"That's a common theme with urban legends. Sorry, Kimberli, go on," Ms. Garza said.

"OK. So she went to summer camp in California. That's where I used to live. Anyway, she liked to sneak out of their cabin at night to drink or whatever. The roommate never snitched but didn't like to go with her. One night it was really cold so she snuck back in the cabin. She didn't want to turn on any lights, so she felt around for her jacket in the dark."

"Oh, I heard this one," someone commented.

"She goes back in the day and the roommate is dead and it says, aren't you glad you didn't turn on the light," someone else finished.

Kimberli's green eyes flashed.

"I heard it too, but it was college dorm," Garrett said.

Kimberli tried to kick him under the table. He grinned at her.

"Ok, settle down," Ms. Garza said. "That's how these things go. Maybe it started as a warning for young girls away from home to keep an eye out for each other, not to sneak off where you shouldn't be."

"No! This one really happened," Kimberli said.

"I heard one about our woods," a voice came from the direction of the door at the back of the room. Everyone turned to see Lindsey standing in the open doorway.

"Um, Miss Pyre? Is that right?" Ms. Garza said.

She nodded her head.

"Please sit down and tell us about our woods."

Lindsey sat in an empty chair closest to the door. "I haven't seen it myself or anything. I looked around this summer but never found it. They say there's a cave somewhere near the canyons that you can hear screaming coming out of and sometimes see misty apparitions in the area. One of the protesters told me this summer that it's not just a cave but a vortex where spirits and other inter-dimensional beings, like aliens, travel in and out of our dimension."

The room went as silent as a tomb.

"Yeah, I heard about a cave, too. But I heard that some crazy guy threw little kids down it in like the forties or something, and now the entire woods is haunted," a boy in the front of the room said, breaking the awkwardness.

Mumbles of agreement came from around the room.

"It would be interesting to find proof," Ms. Garza said.

"I'm working on it," Lindsey said.

Ms. Garza nodded her head thoughtfully, "Let us know what you find out. I'd love to know. Keep thinking about urban legends you know. You can go to my blog and add a story for extra credit. For now, we are going to play a game. I'm going to tell you three stories; you guess which one is the true one, got it?"

The guessing game continued for the rest of the period. It was the least boring English Language Arts class that Nate had ever had. Judging by the smiles and excited participation most everyone felt the same way. The bell rang and students started getting up.

"Hold on, everyone. I dismiss you, not the bell." The class settled down again. "Check the website for tonight's reading assignment. I will know if you didn't read the material, so spare us the drama and read it." She paused. "OK, get out of here. See you tomorrow."

"Hey, I have football, but we can play video games online later or something," Nate said to Garrett as they filed out of class.

"Yeah, that sounds good. I have to work for a couple of hours, so maybe like around 9?" Garrett asked.

"Yeah."

Lindsey pushed between the two of them and sauntered down the hall without a word. Nate almost forgot where he was going.

"Hi, Garrett. How was your last bit of summer? I've missed seeing you in our pool," Kimberli said.

"Oh, hi, Kimberli."

"Who's your new friend?" she said as she looked Nate up and down.

"This is Nate. His family just moved here."

"Hi, Nate. My family has been here like just as long as Garrett's, so if you need someone to show you around just let me know. I should give you my number so you can text me if you want."

Sophia faded in from behind Kimberli "Hi, Nate."

"Hey, Sophia. How's it going?"

Kimberli clicked her tongue. "You know her?"

"Sort of," Nate said.

"Well, she's pretty new, too," Kimberli said.

"Uh, yeah, well I'm OK," Nate said. "I gotta go, I got practice. Talk you later." Nate turned and was swept down the hall with the rush of kids.

"He's really cute," Kimberli said staring in the direction Nate had headed.

"His little sister is going to try out for the squad," Sophia said.

"How do you know?"

"We're in the same ballet class."

Kimberli huffed.

"Well, on that note, I gotta go, too. Later," Garrett said, glad to move away.

He decided to cut through the back parking lot of the school to get to the store. The new asphalt of the parking lot looked inviting, but rocks scattered the smooth surface like open traps. If his wheel caught, he'd wipe for sure. His tender left elbow reminded him that it might not be worth it, and he decided to keep his skateboard hooked under his arm. The wind had picked up, and he knew he didn't need the added challenge. Asphalt and concrete grabbed differently than snow, and he hadn't figured out how to predict it yet.

There was a storm blowing in and the sky turned the color of ripe blueberries. The cloud cover was thick and dark enough to make the parking lot lights come on. Trees bent in the wind, leaves not yet turned for fall blew free and skittered through the air.

A strong feeling of eyes on him made him pause. He looked around, and nothing seemed out of ordinary. The skater kids, the real skater kids, were always trying to show him up. It would be just like them to lurk back here to make fun of him if he wiped out. He hadn't earned his way into their group yet, and he wasn't even sure he wanted to.

A boy stepped out from the corner of the building.

"Excuse me!" the boy hollered. "Can you help me?"

Garrett looked down at his phone to pause the music. He jumped when he looked back up to see the kid had covered the distance between them and was standing right in front of him. He looked to be about twelve and was dressed too warm for the day, even with a rainstorm blowing in. Garrett looked down on the top of the kid's head. The wind blew his bright blonde hair across his face, but Garrett could see his skin was pale.

"Oh, hey!" Garrett said taking an involuntary step back.

"I seem to have lost my house keys, and I need you to take me to your house to use the phone," the kid said.

There was something off about this kid. Maybe he was special needs. Autistic or something.

"You can use my cell," Garrett said.

"No, I have to go to your house," the kid said.

For a second or two Garrett felt compelled to take this strange kid home, but it passed as fast as it came.

"Uh, I don't think so," Garrett said.

The kid reached out to grab Garrett's arm. Garrett pulled back as if it would burn him. He suddenly felt scared. Scared of this weird little kid. His gut told him to move.

"What the fig? Get lost, freak!"

"No! You have to take me to your home!"

Garrett didn't reply. He dropped his board and took off with a powerful thrust. Remembering how fast the kid had covered the distance between them earlier, he wasn't sure if he was a safe distance, but curiosity won out. Looking back, all he saw was an empty parking lot. His stomach twisted and his breakfast threatened to make an encore.

*Did that just happen?*

There had been something not right with the kid. He couldn't be sure, and it should have been the first thing he noticed, but he was almost certain there was something wrong with that kid's eyes. Very wrong.

# CHAPTER SIX

The day had been torturous. Nate spent the second night in a row chasing decent sleep. Every time he caught it he had strange dreams about caves that screamed and spoke through the opening. He could hardly focus on anything except the clock, even though it seemed to stand still. He'd been asked if he was all right at least one hundred times. Football practice had been brutal. It took everything he had to keep his energy level up. His muscles complained and begged for sleep.

His jaw tightened when he got to the gym and cheer tryouts were going strong. His parents asked him to stay and walk Missy home. It wasn't clear if it was because it would be late or if they were worried she wouldn't make the cut. If it was the latter, then they didn't know Missy very well. He sat heavily on the bleachers and wished he hadn't forgotten his earphones at home in the blur of the morning. Now he'd have to listen to the cheers that Kimberli screamed at a group of girls.

Her face bunched up, and like a snake unhinging its jaw, her mouth opened extra wide as she shouted. After the girls repeated the chant to her satisfaction, Kimberli turned it over to Sophia and two others to show the choreography that went with the cheers.

All Nate could gather was that the girls had to learn the moves quickly and then perform the whole thing in groups of three. That would take forever.

Embrace the Suck, he thought.

He was about to wait outside the gym when he felt a not so soft punch to his aching bicep. The group of football players he had been eating lunch with gathered around him. Leave it to these guys to reveal once again that his situational awareness needed some serious work.

"Are you trying to learn some new football moves?" asked the boy who had taunted Nate on the first day he tried out. His name turned out to be Dillan, and he was just as obnoxious off the field.

"Ha, ha, very funny. No. I'm waiting for my sister."

"Dude, is that your sister?" another boy named Ethan asked.

"Oh yeah, she's a hottie," Dillan said.

"Shut up, man," Nate said.

"No, I'm serious. I think we should hook up." Dillan moved his hips in a grinding motion.

Nate stood up, "I'm serious, too."

"Just kidding, man. No need to get your panties in a bunch."

"Whatever," Nate grumbled and sat back down.

"Knock it off, Dillan. What the hell is wrong with you? Come on, let's get out of here before Coach Cruella tosses us out," Bryce said.

Nate smirked. The cheer coach was looking their way with a disapproving stare. She had short cropped hair that was graying in a way that left a dark streak on one side much like the famous dog hater, Cruella Deville. She gave Nate one last shot of venom as a warning after the other guys left him alone.

Nate began to see a light at the end of the tunnel, the time to announce the girls who had made the cut had arrived. When each girl's name was called they squealed and jumped around like they had just won a new car. Missy was the last Junior Varsity girl to be announced. She jumped and squealed toward Nate. Her excited hug nearly knocked him off the bleacher.

"I told you I would make it!"

"Yeah, yeah. Never doubted you. Can we go now?" he asked as he peeled her off of himself.

"Yes. But I told Sophia she could walk with us, OK? Some creeper was hanging out the other day when she left practice."

"A creeper? What kind of creeper?"

"Um, yeah, some kid like harassed her."

"Harassed her?"

"What are you? Some kind of jock parrot? Ask her yourself if you're so interested."

Sophia stepped up next to Missy and gave her a hug. "I told you! You were amazing!"

"Thanks for all your help, Sophia!"

"Excuse me, I hate to interrupt this love fest, but I really want to go home," Nate said.

They both turned and looked at him as if they just realized he was there. Sophia blushed, Missy looked annoyed. "It's not my fault stuff went late."

"Girls! Girls! Bring it in!" the coach yelled.

Nate had about all he could take of squealing girls. He grabbed his stuff and headed for the hallway outside the gym to finishing waiting. He was relieved to see that the building wasn't as deserted as he thought it would be this long after school let out. Mostly construction crews finishing the work that had yet to be done.

Tossing his stuff on the floor, he slid down the wall and sat next to the pile of backpack and gym bag. He hoped this wouldn't take much longer; it was getting dark. As much as he hated to admit it, the thought of walking home in the dark was not the least bit appealing.

The kids that had been on his porch wanted to come in just like the kid that Sophia encountered. Somebody was running around punking people. Maybe they were trying to rob everyone. People are pretty willing to help kids. Evil minds could use that to their advantage. You let them in to use the phone because they are just kids. Then BAM, next thing you know, you're tied up in the closet, and your house is picked clean.

A man in work clothes popped his head around the corner making Nate start.

"Hey, kid? Can you tell them to wait about five minutes before they use the front doors? We are just finishing fixin' the broken one." He jabbed a thumb toward the gym.

"Yeah, sure."

"Thanks," and he disappeared back around the corner.

It would probably take the girls longer than five minutes anyway. He pulled his math book from his backpack and thumbed through the pages assigned for homework. A review of stuff from last year that shouldn't take him long. Yanking a spiral notebook out, he got to work.

He was just about done with the third and final page when the gym doors banged open, and girls flooded out. Nate jumped to his feet to avoid being trampled. Missy was beaming and sporting a pair of black and green warmups with Dark Pine Hills emblazoned down one leg and matching jacket.

"Look, Nate! I got my warmups!"

"Awesome. Can we get out of here now?"

"Yes," she hissed.

"Thanks for letting me walk with you guys," Sophia said.

"No problem. Some kid scared you?"

"Yeah, it was weird. I was the last one out of practice and he was knocking on that door." She gestured to the door at the far end of the corridor. "He knocked and yelled at me to let him in. He didn't really do anything, just creeped me out."

"Creeped you out?"

Sophia blushed and looked at the floor, "I-I can't explain it. There was just something creepy about him, you know."

A loud crescendo of breaking glass made everyone jump.

"What was that?" Missy asked with eyes wide.

"I don't know," Nate said.

They rushed toward the noise with the rest of the crowd. A man in a hard hat stopped them with outstretched arms.

"Kids! Kids, stay back!"

Mr. Greene, the high school principal, was suddenly there. His face flushed, and sweating more than usual. His belly forever pushing his trousers down his hips, and he had a habit of continually hitching them up. But now he yanked them up with such force Nate cringed. A furiously-whispered conversation between him, the construction worker, and the cheer coach ensued. Mr. Greene sent spittle flying over the head of the coach.

"OK, kids. There's been an accident, and we will need you all to go back around. I'll unlock the eighth-grade entrance, and you can all go out that way. If you have a ride waiting you can walk around to the parking lot, OK?" Mr. Greene said.

He led the way and the cheer coach herded the crowd from behind. Sirens wailed, getting louder.

"I hope we can see what happened when we walk around to the front," Missy said.

"My sister, the busybody," Nate said, trying to lighten the mood. Sophia gave him a weak smile in return.

It took a few minutes to get everyone out of the exit. Mr. Greene didn't know that the outer doors got chained shut at night by the custodians. The heavy locks and chains rattled as the custodian worked them out from the door handles. When the doors sprung open the crowd rushed out into the darkening school yard. Blue and red lights strobed eerily off the trees and building.

Kimberli maneuvered her way through the crowd to push up next to Nate.

"Scary, huh?"

Nate didn't acknowledge her. Maybe if he ignored her she would go away, like a wasp.

"Your sister was like really good at tryouts. She's totally got the moves. She might even be good enough to take like captain. When I'm graduated, of course."

Missy leaned over Nate. "Thanks, Kimberli!"

A buzzing in his pocket saved him. He pulled out his phone and checked the screen.

"Mom says we are supposed to go home with Sophia's dad. They must have heard about the accident, I guess," he said to Missy.

"What about my dad?" Sophia asked.

"We're supposed to wait for him. He's going to pick us all up," Missy said.

Kimberli clicked her tongue, "My mom is already here; she can like give you a ride home if you don't want to wait for Sophia's dad."

"No, it's cool. My mom would have a heart attack if we do that," Nate said.

"Why?" Kimberli demanded.

"She's paranoid about us taking rides unless the driver has her permission," Missy said, rolling her eyes.

They rounded the building and the sight of an ambulance, fire truck, and two police cars nipped the conversation. Mr. Greene had stopped on the sidewalk and ushered kids onto the newly laid sod to cut a direct path to the parking lot without passing the front of the building. They still passed close enough to take in some of the action. The protesters who stationed themselves at the open space across from the school lowered their signs and silently gathered in a curious group.

A heavy, older man in a school district security officer uniform and a paramedic were leaning over the same man who had told Nate to wait before using the main doors. He was sitting on a planter, and a rough blanket was draped over his hunched shoulders. He elbows pressed into his knees, and he was squeezing his head in his hands as if he thought his skull might come apart.

"I can't understand it. We were done. He was tightening the last bolt. I left him alone so I could start cleaning up. Why did I do that?" he cried.

"It's alright," the paramedic said.

"I heard kids ask to come in. He told them to wait. They begged. I- the next thing I hear is the door crash. I run over there and seen him pinned under that huge piece of glass. He was..." his voice trailed off.

"Are the kids still here? Maybe they can tell us what happened," the district security officer said.

"I-I don't know. I don't remember seeing them when I got there. They must have taken off. It sounded like one or two boys. Oh God, someone has to call his wife!"

Nate looked at Sophia. She looked pale. A horn honked. The kids looked over to see a man leaning out the driver's side window of a bright yellow Mini Cooper with part of the black racing stripes missing.

"There's my dad," Sophia said.

Nate was skeptical that they could all fit, his gym bag was bigger than the car. Mr. Lewis hopped out and opened the back hatch which was roomier than it looked. Not that it mattered, Nate would have squeezed in any way he could rather than walk home in the gathering darkness.

Mr. Lewis dropped them off to an empty house. Nate made a quick check of the doors, jiggling the handles to be sure they were locked. He peered out the big patio doors onto the dark yard and down into the canyon. In the gloom, it was easy to imagine a cave where ghosts and monsters came and went at will. No wonder no one wanted to go into the woods.

Except for Lindsey. She was brave enough to go in and look for the cave.

To his relief, the screech of the garage door announced the arrival of one or the other of his parents. It was his dad with Chinese take-out from the place that made everything without gluten. Mel came in a few minutes later and they ate to Missy recounting, moment by moment, her rise to cheerleader fame.

After eating, Nate went up to his room to read the pages that Ms. Garza assigned for homework. It didn't take long, and he quickly turned to his Navy SEAL book.

Lying among the still unpacked boxes he could hear snippets of his parents' conversation float up the stairs. As usual, it was a boring discussion about the benefits for Nate and Missy of being bi-racial on college applications.

Nate never really gave it much thought or considered himself to be biracial. David Camden was white, Melita Camden was Italian and African-American. Mel was technically the biracial person in the family; he was more like the steak sauce with 57 spices. But whatever made them happy and shipping him off to college the second he was able to go seemed to be their number one source of happiness.

Nobody had bothered to ask him if he was interested in college. He was OK at school and would definitely like to play college football, but four more years of hitting the books did not seem appealing.

Football. He thought about the guys on his team. If he wasn't on the football team he would have eaten his lunch alone or at a table with strangers. As usual, football saved the day. Too bad it didn't work that way for everyone. Cooper couldn't get his knee fixed because his family didn't have insurance. If they couldn't go to the doctor for big things like torn ACLs, did it mean that they couldn't go for things like strep throat?

He was thinking about how that would be when the boys who had been on his porch wandered into his thoughts. It had been a weird experience, the weirdest he had ever had. How did they disappear like that? Then, maybe, one of the boys had tried to get Sophia to let him into the school.

Nate envisioned a gang of white-haired boys materializing out of a cave in the nearby woods. He shook the thought off as ridiculous. More likely they were part of a gang of thieves working the isolated neighborhood. They probably figured that a ritzy area like this one would have good stuff.

Somewhere in his detective work he must have drifted off to sleep because he woke up later to a silent and dark house. Drool soaked a spot on his pillow.

"Gross," he mumbled and wiped his mouth with the back of his hand as he flipped his pillow over.

Lying back down, he heard what must have woken him in the first place, a light tapping at the window. The tapping grew louder and more insistent.

"Hey, kid. We still need to come in," harshly whispered through the shut blinds.

Nate stumbled out of bed and headed for the window. *It must be those guys from the other day. What did they need? Oh, yeah, the phone, to call for money to go to the store. No, the market.*

Nate froze mid-shuffle. He looked to his cell phone in the charger on his bedside table. 3:15 glowed on the screen. He rubbed his eyes, was he dreaming?

"Let us in," the voice hissed from the other side of the window.

Looking around the room he remembered that he was in his new house. He felt gooseflesh creep across his arms and adrenaline shot arrows from his gut. With the vaulted ceilings below him, his second-story window had to be at least twenty feet off the ground with no ledge. Whoever, or whatever, was outside that window wasn't here to rob them.

# CHAPTER SEVEN

A yelp escaped his throat, and he leaped back, knocking over moving boxes. David rushed into the room.

"What happened?" His graying hair stuck out in all directions as if he had been tossing and turning on his pillow.

"I-I think someone threw rocks at my window. I tripped in the dark."

David went to the window, and Nate pulled himself up inside and braced for the worst. The blinds flew up with the force of David's hard tug. They clattered together like dry bones to reveal nothing but the night. David pressed his face close to the window and searched the yard and street below.

"Well, there's nothing there now. You were probably dreaming."

"Yeah, probably."

His dad studied him for a few seconds.

"Are you feeling OK, son? You look a little pale."

By this time, Mel had come into the room. She crossed over to Nate and pressed the back of her hand to his forehead.

"You're ice cold!"

"Am I? I feel fine. Like Dad said, I must have been dreaming."

Mel wrapped her light robe around herself as if she were cold too. She opened her mouth to say something but swallowed it and left the room.

"You need to get this room unpacked, buddy," David said as he headed back to his bedroom.

Nate lay awake for the rest of the night listening for any strange sound. He half expected the boys or whatever they were, to pop right into his room. He didn't think he had been dreaming. There was no way to know what they were, but he knew they were not normal kids. Ghosts, or vampires maybe, but he also knew there was no such thing, right?

Nate had never been more grateful when the daybreak singing of birds replaced the night sounds. He was the last one down for breakfast. Mel was already gone. David poured a cup of coffee and Missy poked at a yogurt.

"All I'm saying is that a yogurt cup is not enough fuel for the whole day," David said.

"Dad! I'm trying to cut down on carbs," Missy said.

"At least let me make you some toast,"

"I'll take toast," Nate said.

"Hey, slowpoke. Fine, but we have to leave in like ten minutes. I'll put it in, you butter it."

Nate nodded and dropped into a chair at the table. David started the toaster and went into the home office to gather his paperwork.

"Technically, some people consider yogurt a carb," Nate said.

"No one asked you."

"Hey, are you sure you didn't see anyone on the porch the other night?" he asked.

She let out an annoyed sigh. "I said no." She was about to call him a name but when she looked at him she stopped. "Are you sick?"

"No, I just didn't sleep very good."

"Oh." She hesitated. There was a heaviness in his voice she had never heard there before. "Sorry."

The glimpse of sympathy surprised him, "Wait for me after school, OK?"

She clicked her tongue. "Why?"

"I don't know. I just don't want you to walk home alone."

She raised her eyebrows. "I don't think I heard you right. You want to walk home together?"

"Yeah, I do."

There was that thing in his voice again. "OK, I'll wait."

"Good," he said. He had no idea what was happening to him. Maybe it was his imagination, or hey, there could be a gas leak in this house causing him to hallucinate. But the feeling of dread that overwhelmed him last night was undeniable.

"Come on, guys! Let's go!" David called.

Nate needed to talk to Sophia. Did she and the guy working on the door see the same kids, or whatever, as him? The kids in each encounter had asked to come in. He had to know, but how could he bring it up to her without sounding like a total nut job.

*Oh, hey Sophia, did that creepy kid float up to your window to harass you? Yes! Me too. Got any extra garlic*?

He shook his head and grunted.

"Hey buddy, are you OK?" David asked from the driver's seat.

"Oh, uh, yeah. Just going over plays in my head. First game tomorrow."

"You'll do fine. Just remember, it's only a game."

"Yeah," his annoyance burned the back of his throat and took his attention.

He'd seen other parents build a fan-club for their kid that played sports. They crowded the sideline in matching shirts with the kid's name, cheering and holding up poster board signs. Window stickers with the kid's number and name adorned their cars, advertising their pride of their offspring everywhere they traveled. But not his. They acted like this was a passing phase Nate was traveling through until he found, what? What exactly did they expect from him?

"It's going to be so fun!" Missy said from the backseat. "I can't wait to be out there with my squad. We get to do a routine at halftime and I get to do front handsprings. It's so awesome!"

Nate rolled his eyes. David gave him a light tap on the thigh and smiled.

"I'll be there. Mom has a meeting that ends late, but she'll get there as soon as she can. Before halftime, I'm sure."

"Dad, did you hear anything about the guy that got hurt working on the school?" Nate asked.

"Like what?"

"I don't know. Like what caused the door to fall."

"No. Nothing."

"Seriously, do we have to talk about it?" Missy asked.

The car pulled up to the curb in front of the school and Nate opened his door before the car came to full stop. He didn't wait for Missy. He slammed the car door shut with a loud thud and took long strides across the dew-soaked grass.

Each grade level had a separate entrance to keep the chaos to a minimum and the younger kids from getting mowed down. Nate took the quickest way to the ninth grade entrance on the west side of the building leaving Missy to walk by herself to her entrance on the east side.

Standing a head taller than most everyone made scanning the crowd for Sophia easier. Several teachers pushed through the throngs of kids to use the student entrance. The main entrance was off-limits until repairs were done.

He spotted her at the far end of the grounds talking to a woman he didn't recognize. If he was going to bring it up, it had to be now. He might not have the guts to do it later and his chances of getting her alone like this again were slim. Girls tended to travel in packs. He'd figure out how to approach the subject when he got there. Nate cracked the knuckles on his right hand and headed Sophia's way.

As he got closer, he realized that Sophia was crying. Round water spots from tears stained the green DP decal on her cheer uniform top. He hesitated, considering turning back.

He eyed the woman. She had the same green eyes as Sophia. Her dark hair tied up in a loose bun and her tight jeans tucked into black high-heeled boots. The bones of her skull were visible on her face. He hadn't seen her before at the school. If the heavy makeup was any sign, she probably wasn't a teacher. The woman shifted her gaze to him and narrowed her eyes. Sophia turned around to follow where she was looking.

"Nate, what are you doing?" Sophia asked.

"I'm-um-I'm-I'm Nate," he said. He walked over and extended his hand to the woman.

The woman looked at his hand as if it was covered with worms. "Think about what I said, Sophie. You know it's true. I'll call you later. I gotta go."

She gave Nate one last glare and crossed the street where a car sat waiting for her.

"You OK?" Nate asked.

"Yeah." She dabbed under her eyes, but her makeup was beyond help.

"Who was that?"

Sophia cast her eyes down. "My mom."

"Your mom?"

"Please don't tell anyone. It's so embarrassing."

"Embarrassing? Everyone's parents are embarrassing."

"No, you don't understand. My mom is sick."

He tilted his head to the side like a dog trying to understand his master's words. "She's sick?"

Sophia sighed as if it were her last breath. "She's a drug addict, OK. She started with pain pills from a car accident a few years ago and never stopped. She just got out of jail over her last stint and found us. She's constantly pulling me into her drama. I'm so sick of it!" She snapped her mouth shut to stop the words from spilling out.

Nate wasn't sure what to say. He had never known anyone who even knew someone who had been to jail or was a drug addict.

"It's OK. I won't tell anyone."

"Guess you think I'm a big loser and my family is a bunch of freaks."

"No. I think you have problems just like everyone else at this school. They all act like their lives are golden, but everyone has crap. Even me."

"You? Mister super athlete who lives in a killer house, has great parents, who all the girls are crazy for?" She stopped herself. "I'm sorry. I didn't mean to take it out on you."

"It's OK. Believe it or not, my parents drive me nuts. Sometimes I think there was a mix-up at the hospital, or maybe I'm just a social experiment for them."

"I'll trade you," she said.

"Your dad seems like a good guy."

Sophia shrugged. "He is. He's tried really hard to make up for my mom." She tossed her head back. "Uunh, I'm a hot mess. I can't let anyone see me this way."

"I can go get Missy and your other friends to help."

"Oh God, no! That is exactly who can't see me. Nate, you have no idea how evil those girls can be."

Nate pinched his eyebrows together. Evil? He thought about Missy. She could be self-centered and snotty, but evil? The current territory felt oddly dangerous and retreat was looking like a good option. Then he remembered why he had approached her.

"We could go to the convenience store and use their bathroom, but we gotta hurry."

They strode across the parking lot and crossed the street to the tiny store. Nate didn't expect Garrett to be working behind the counter. The boys made eye contact.

"What?" Garrett mouthed the word.

Nate shrugged.

He and Sophia went straight to the back of the store and Sophia went into the ladies room. Nate leaned against the wall and stuck his hands in his pockets to keep from cracking his knuckles.

"Nate, thanks for coming with me. I feel so stupid," she said through the door.

"It's OK. Hey, I wanted to ask you something."

"Yeah?"

"That kid you saw the other day, the one that wanted to come inside?"

"Yeah?"

"Well, I think I saw him too. Only he wasn't alone and, well, his eyes were messed up, or something."

Sophia's eyes widened as she looked into the mirror. She froze mid-swipe of mascara. "We may have seen the same kid. Any idea who it is?"

The bathroom door swished open and much to Nate's surprise, Sophia stepped out looking like she had not shed a single tear. She ran her hands over the front and back of her uniform to smooth it out.

"There was something so weird about that kid," she said. "When did you see him?"

"He came to my house with another kid."

"Your house? What did they want?"

"To come in."

She sucked in her breath.

An older gentleman wearing khaki hiking pants and a fedora stood near the entrance. He leaned heavily on a walking stick.

"OK, kids! Your bell rings in less than two minutes. See you later, Garrett. Thanks for opening," he said.

Sophia and Nate were almost across the parking lot when Garrett called to them from behind, "Hey guys! Hang on a minute," he jogged to catch up with them. "Sorry, but I overheard you talking."

Nate's surprise gave way to trying to plan a lame explanation. The conversation with Sophia had gone without him sounding too crazy. He didn't need Garrett thinking he had lost his mind, but he wasn't sure he could pull it off a second time.

Garrett leaned in. "I think I may have seen the kid, too."

"What?" Sophia asked, her mouth hanging open.

"I don't know, man. He came up to me out here and wanted to come home with me. I got freaked out and I booked it out of here. Kid just gave me the creeps."

"Come home with you?" Sophia asked.

"The kids I saw had really weird eyes. I think," Nate said.

"I didn't get a good look at his eyes," Garrett said.

"Couldn't it just be kids with some contacts, you know? Or maybe dilated eyes? Drugs, maybe?" she cast her eyes down.

"Maybe," Nate said. He would not offer the experience he had with these boys whispering into his second-story bedroom window. Here in the light of day with his friends it seemed possible he had simply dreamed it. Not just possible, but likely.

"I don't know. I saw something like this on the show Paranormal Files the other day," Garrett said.

"I love that show!" Sophia said. "I saw it last night, and they were talking about this mysterious paranormal website that's made by a ghost! Do you think those kids are ghosts?"

Nate did not like the direction the conversation had taken. "Hold on, guys. What are you saying?"

Garrett shook his head, "Nah, nothing that cool would happen around here."

Sophia shrugged. "I know. It's most likely kids pulling pranks or something."

The bell rang and they entered the rush of students. Garrett and Sophia went to the lockers on the right and Nate attempted to navigate the flow of kids to the left. Like Nate, Garrett was a head taller than most of the kids, but he was about to be swallowed by the wave.

"Hey dude, later!" Garrett called.

Something Sophia said earlier dawned on him, "Sophia, wait! What? Crazy? For me?"

She stuck her arm over the crowd and waved to him.

Nate was feeling 100% better. Of course, they were just weird kids with weird contacts out trying to punk people. He had only dreamed they were at his window. Hadn't his dad pulled up the blinds and nothing was there? The construction accident was just that, an accident. No weird ghost kids had caused the door to fall on anyone. He felt the weight of it lift off his shoulders. Finally, time to get back to normal and football.

Sophia knelt in front of her locker and slipped her homework out of her backpack. The interaction with her mom had wiped her out; even her bones felt tired. The last thing she wanted to do was go to class. Maybe she could fake sick. The approaching sound of giggling and rustling cheer skirts said it was too late. Sighing with resignation she slammed her locker shut and fell in with the group.

"Did you guys did see what Mr. Holstren has on today?" Kimberli asked.

"Oh my God, he seriously needs to buy a mirror!"

"Maybe teachers don't make enough money to buy mirrors. Did you see Mr. Greene?"

Sophia was too tired and distracted to join their laughter.

"You're quiet, Sophia," Kimberli said.

All eyes turned on her. The pack waiting to see if the alpha female had called out the weakest member so they could all pounce.

"I just have a headache. I think my time-of-the-month is getting ready to start."

The crowd gave a sympathetic ooh.

"It wouldn't have like anything to do with a certain football player, would it?" Kimberli said.

"What would a football player have to do with my headache?"

The group stopped walking. Kimberli turned to face Sophia and took a step into her personal space.

"You know exactly what I mean. I saw you and Nate leave school this morning."

Sophia swallowed hard. It hadn't dawned on her that being with Nate might be a problem. Kimberli had put dibs on him. He may not know it, but as far as anyone was concerned, they were a couple. That meant hands off for anyone else. Sophia caught Missy's eye. She was watching Sophia carefully.

"Oh. We just happened to be going the same way. I needed something with caffeine and he needed, um-"

"Gum," Missy offered. "My brother's addicted to the stuff."

"Oh. I was like just kidding, Sophia," Kimberli laughed, realizing Missy's connection to Nate. The other girls joined in. "You're so cute," she flipped her blonde ponytail over her shoulder and went into class.

Sophia gave Missy a slight smile. If ballet didn't work out, Sophia figured that the CIA could use somebody with her skills. She could keep cover under the most intense pressure and relationships among girls could be about as dangerous as being a double agent.

Sophia and Missy squeezed hands for a quick second, an unspoken understanding passing between them.

# CHAPTER EIGHT

Linda stretched and her neck popped, signaling it was time to pack it in for the day. Getting lesson plans fleshed out for the next couple of weeks was a satisfying end to a long day. The kids had been wound up over the construction accident that happened the night before.

If she admitted it, the staff was wound up too. The main entrance was taped off while the investigation was ongoing and she was grateful to use a different entrance. It was a horrible thing to think those beautiful glass doors were so heavy that a man was crushed to death by one. She had the irrational vision of them randomly falling off the hinges and crushing any unsuspecting passerby.

She gathered her things and shut off her computer. The corridors were deserted and dark. The only sound was the swish-swish sound her shoes made as she moved along the carpet.

Glancing at her watch, she was surprised to see it was past six. She hadn't intended to stay so late. The vibrating of her cell phone in the front pocket of her slacks startled her. She leaned against the stair railing, she shifted her purse and pulled the phone out.

"Hello?"

Silence.

"Hello?" She pulled the phone away from her ear to check for bars, no problem there. She put the phone back to her ear.

"Lin?" a man's voice.

Her chest tightened. "How did you get this number?"

"It doesn't matter. I need to talk to you."

"I don't care. How did you get this number?"

"Lin, I miss you. Please, can't we just talk?"

"No. I told you never to contact me!"

"I just had to see if you are OK. I miss you," he said.

"It is none of your business if I am OK! Don't ever call this number again! I said I never wanted to talk to you again and I meant it! Just leave me alone!" She disconnected the call with shaking fingers.

"Linda, are you all right? I heard shouting." Inna came out into the hallway from her late night in the classroom.

"Oh, Inna. I didn't realize you were here, too."

"Honey, are you OK? You look like you just saw a ghost."

Inna's expression of genuine concern was more than Linda's reserve could withstand. She burst into tears. Inna rushed to her and hugged her tightly. Inna held Linda until the sobs subsided.

"Come back to my room. I just made some really good coffee in my new coffee press. We can talk," Inna said.

Linda sniffed and wiped under her eyes with her fingers. "I'm sorry. I just wasn't..." she sniffed.

"You don't have to be sorry. Come on, coffee makes everything better."

"Thank you, but I really just need to get home. I'm OK now."

"Are you sure?"

"Yes, we'll have that coffee sometime and I'll tell you about it. But now I just need to get home and get some rest."

Inna smiled. "OK, but I'm holding you to that."

"OK, thanks." Linda descended the stairway.

"You sure you're OK?"

"Yes, fine!" she called over her shoulder.

Inna was fairly sure she was anything but.

Inna went back into her classroom and poured herself a cup of coffee. She was lucky, caffeine never really affected her ability to sleep. She sat back down at her computer and returned to revamping her original thirteen colonies presentation. The plan had been for the kids to watch it online for homework tonight, but when she looked it over to upload it, she realized that it was so old that it looked like it had been created in one of the colonies.

Maybe hot coffee wasn't such a great idea. The air conditioning went off promptly two hours after the dismissal bell and it was already getting warm. Lifting her hair off the back of her neck she searched her messy desktop looking for the hair clip she was sure was there. Above the shuffling of papers, she thought she heard a light knock on the door. She stopped and listened. It was quiet. She crossed to the door and opened it.

There was no one there.

She peered down the darkened corridor, each way, but saw no one. She strained her ears. Deathly silent, not even the usual night noise of the vacuum being run by the night crew.

She thought she heard a door click shut somewhere but could not tell exactly where the sound had come from. She didn't detect any movement in the corridor. The darkened stillness of the building felt alien. Inna was suddenly aware of the size of the building and all the ways someone could have entered undetected with the front entrance off limits.

What if a crazed ax murderer had come in during the day and hidden only to come out at night to hunt?

Or a deranged student had been in hiding, waiting to exact revenge on an unsuspecting teacher. Based on the news stories in the recent past that one was a little too realistic.

She chided herself. She'd been alone in schools at night before, even in questionable neighborhoods, and never been frightened.

Returning to her desk, she picked up her cell phone. She wanted to take a photo of a paper worksheet she wanted her students to use. The school frowned on too many photocopies, so she decided to post it as a picture to the homework site. Students could use up their own ink to print it out. She started to email the photo to herself when she noticed a "no service" notification at the top of the screen. She'd a perfectly fine signal a few minutes earlier. That was the problem with technology, unpredictable. It always flaked out in the most inconvenient times.

There was a flatbed network-connected scanner in the teachers' workroom on the main floor in the office. She had never used it, but at the start of the year in-service, the school technologist had given them a quick overview of how to use it. It seemed easy enough.

She took the worksheet and went down the sprawling main stairway to the office. The sparse lighting made the area slightly unrecognizable; she was used to seeing it in the well-lit daylight. She made a brisk trip through the maze of secretary desks to the small back room.

She flicked the switch on the workroom wall and bright fluorescent light flooded the small room. A computer, a scanner, a copy machine, and floor to ceiling shelves of office supplies greeted her. An image of herself and the room reflected back at her in the lone window. This room had a door with outside access for only one purpose, escape. Thank you, Columbine.

Not fully over her dark thoughts, she moved across the room and checked the door. Finding it securely locked, she settled down at the computer. Her fingers barely touched the keyboard when she heard what sounded like light knocking on the door. She stopped. Sure enough, there it was again.

Someone had seen her in the brightly lit room through the window. Her heart rhythm jumped up.

A more insistent knock made her jump like a cat.

She crept to the door and leaned her ear against it.

"Hello?" she called. The light giggling of children answered her.

"You are not supposed to be on school grounds after dark!"

More giggling.

"I mean it. I will call the cops!"

Silence.

Inna reached over and pulled the cord for the window shades. They dropped with a bang that made her cringe.

Harder knocking now.

"Ma'am, can we come in and use the phone?"

It sounded like a boy.

She parted the blinds and peered out. Two young boys were standing in front of the door. One looked old enough to be in middle school, and the other boy was probably a younger sibling, but she didn't recognize either one. Both boys had very blond hair, almost white, that stood out against the darkness of the abandoned school yard.

The teacher in her kicked in. "Can I help you guys? Are you here with your parents?" she called through the closed door.

"We need to use the phone. Can we come in?" the older boy asked.

"Who are you with? Why are you here so late?"

"We need to come in and help you. We could clean desks," he said.

Inna felt confused. What kind of kids want to clean desks? Her students knew they used tables, not desks.

"Who are you boys with?"

"May we come in and use the phone to call our parents? We need permission to be here."

The doorknob jiggled.

"No," she said much quieter than she intended.

The older boy took a step toward the window and into the light that spilled out. Her breath caught in her chest. He had lifeless ebony eyes. Shark eyes. The blackness swallowed the entire socket.

"Let us in, please. We need your permission," the younger boy said in a deep voice that did not match his body.

Inna dropped the blinds and let her breath out in a yelp. Sprinting out of the room she grabbed the phone off the nearest desk and ducked under it. She dialed the school district's security office. Thank God the number was on a sticker on the phone.

"Security," a reassuring voice answered.

"I'm at Dark Pine Hills Academy and there are some..." she hesitated. Some what?

"Ma'am?"

"I'm a teacher here and there are some kids trying to get into the building." She knew it sounded ridiculous even as she said it.

The voice at the end of the line hesitated. "You mean they're trying to break in?"

"No, I don't think so. They are just running around and knocking on doors. They don't have any..." She hesitated again. What was she going to say? Eyeballs? They'd put her on administrative leave. "Any permission to be here. They acted in an aggressive manner when I confronted them."

"Are you hurt, ma'am?"

"No, no. I just know they aren't supposed to be here."

"OK, I'm dispatching someone to you now. I see you are calling from the office. I'm going to turn on the security camera until the officer gets to you, OK?"

Every area of the school was equipped with video recording devices that could be activated in the case of an emergency and monitored from the security office. Thanks again, Columbine. Inna quickly stood up, how would it look if she were cowering under the desk?

"I'm monitoring you now, ma'am."

It was not long before she heard the main door to the office open.

"District security, Officer Baldwin," a voice called out.

"Yes, hi, I'm Mrs. Kerpin."

As relieved as she was to have another person with her, she still didn't feel better. The security officer was bigger around his middle than he was tall. His wrinkled and somewhat gnarled hands rested on his nonexistent hips. The gun peeking out from under the eaves of his belly was the only thing that indicated he might be able to protect her.

"I checked around the building and had central run the cameras. We only saw you and the two night custodians in the building and no one outside. The kids must have hauled it out of here after you talked to them."

"Oh, um, OK."

"Did you recognize the kids?"

"No, I don't think they are students here."

"I can walk you to your car after I get a quick statement from you, alright?"

Maybe he wasn't an intimidating figure, but he was a living breathing body to walk with in the dark parking lot. "Yes, that would be great."

After the paperwork, they tracked down the custodians. Neither of them had seen or heard anything.

Inna could tell by the way they looked at her they weren't sure about her story. Officer Baldwin listened carefully and stood with the same stance he had in the office, but he pushed his eyeglasses up to balance on the top of his barren head as if they were somehow obscuring his view of the scenario.

"Well, if they were here, they seem to be gone now," he said.

"If?" Inna said.

"I mean, I'm sure you saw somebody, but they're not here now."

"OK." She smoothed her auburn hair away from her face.

"Come on, we're done here. I'll walk you out to your car."

Once inside her car, she locked all the doors. Driving out of the parking lot, she jerked her foot on the accelerator harder than she had intended and her wheels squealed in protest. She looked in her rearview mirror to see Officer Baldwin standing under the street light with the same suspicious stance. He must think she was some kind of hysterical person, a teacher about to crack. The stress making her imagine kids were coming to get her.

She wished it was her imagination, but she knew better. Those eyes. It had to be a trick of light or contacts, maybe. It had felt strange. Supernatural was the term that came to mind. She laughed out loud to the empty car. Ridiculous.

But those eyes. They had been darker than dark. It was if they were absorbing the surrounding light. She felt her will being sucked into them right along with the light. Her eyes darted from the road to the sidewalk to her mirrors, half expecting those boys to be standing there, illuminated by her headlights. Or worse, sitting in her back seat.

She did not turn off her car or unlock the doors until her garage door sealed shut behind her. Her purse, school stuff, and lunch bag would have to wait. She sprinted into the house and bolted the door behind her.

Inna flew around the house checking windows and doors and turning on lights. She closed the door to the basement and pushed a small bench in front of it. No way was she going down to the unfinished basement. If her husband wasn't out of town, he would think she had lost her mind. Maybe she had.

She turned the television on for the company. *Dang it, why didn't they have a dog*? This is why people owned dogs. Forget the allergies. The protection would be worth some sneezing. Inna curled up in the armchair and turned down the volume of the television. She had to be able to hear if anyone knocked.

A serious headache blossomed in her temples. A picture of the boys filled her mind's eye. Those eyes.

We need permission. That's what he said. Those damn eyes were burned into her brain like a cattle brand.

Her stomach tightened, she lurched and threw up on her well-groomed beige carpeting.

# CHAPTER NINE

It was game day. The opener. A day Nate usually felt fired up for. He felt better after he spoke with Sophia and Garrett but the events of the past few days left him feeling unsettled. He'd have to shake the feeling before game time.

Ms. Kerpin had her back to the class, writing out page numbers from their textbook on the whiteboard. She'd told them all to read the intro to chapter two, even though they were on chapter three. When a girl with short red hair tried to inform her of that, she slammed her hand on the desktop making everyone jump. A shrill beep from the intercom interrupted the awkward silence that settled in the room.

"We are on lockdown! Please begin lockdown procedures immediately!" squawked through the speakers.

Kids looked around wide-eyed. There hadn't been an announcement about a drill. Was this the real thing?

Ms. Kerpin spun around. The color drained from her face and Nate felt his adrenaline spike in response.

"Get down in this corner," she growled, pointing behind her desk. She grabbed her keys off the desk, scurried across the room and pulled the door shut. The keys jingled loudly as she tried to lock the door with shaking hands.

Nate moved with the class to the corner and they all squatted down. Girls, and maybe some boys, were whimpering.

"Is this real?" someone whispered.

Ms. Kerpin flipped off the light and came to sit with her students.

"Miss? What's happening?" a boy asked.

"I don't know," she hissed. "Shhh! Make sure your phones are on silent."

Nate's phone was already in silent. His heart beat so hard he could see his shirt move. Ms. Kerpin whispered roll call then they sat in silence.

Kids moved around as quietly as possible to get more comfortable as the minutes ticked by. Nate moved his head around on his neck, trying to keep from getting too stiff.

The locked doorknob jiggled. Everyone stared at it. It jiggled again and Nate felt his muscles tense.

He had been playing out various scenarios in his head. The section of Navy SEAL book he read last night was about having a SEAL's mindset and one of the components was visualization. They envisioned every possible outcome of a mission so that if and when they encountered it on an actual mission, they'd be ready for it. He wasn't sure if he was ready for any of the things he imagined.

The door flew open and Mr. Greene was standing there with his hand on the door knob. "Everyone accounted for?"

"Yes," Ms. Kerpin responded.

He nodded. "All clear."

The room erupted in mumbles and relieved sighs. Ms. Kerpin joined Mr. Greene in the hallway and closed the door partway.

"Guys, one of the protesters lost it!" a kid holding his phone above his head announced.

Ms. Kerpin came back in and walked purposefully to the front of the class.

"We are fine. There was some police action outside the school. We were never in danger. We locked down just as a precaution." She sounded like she was reading from a script.

Nate pulled his phone and did a quick web search. The news story popped up in seconds. A person protesting outside the school pulled a gun and threatened the other protesters. She then attempted to get into the school shouting, "They are here! We have to get out! They'll kill us all!"

The reporter wrote that no one knew what she was talking about. Nate scrolled down. There was a picture of the woman who had blocked their car with a sparkly sign. She'd been arrested and everything was back to normal.

Nate was beginning to wonder just what was normal was in Dark Pine Hills.

By the time the football game got started all the drama was mostly forgotten. A few parents came, mostly elementary school, and picked up their students but for the most part, classes went on as scheduled. A larger than usual crowd for the first game filled the stands and the atmosphere was light.

Dark Pine lost the coin toss and the other team started on defense. Nate's heart pounded in his chest as if he had already run a marathon as he lined up for the first play of the game. He heard Missy yell his name over the other crowd noise.

Bryce called the play. Nate ran his route. The ball found his arms. A small truck crashed into his side before his feet could move. The crowd erupted in cheers.

"I'm gonna grind your head all day," the truck snarled as he lay on top of Nate.

"Good luck, Mac. I only let you catch me this time because it wouldn't be right to blow you out of the water on the first play," Nate replied as he jumped off the ground.

"My name's not Mac."

"Exactly," Nate laughed and turned to trot back to his huddle.

That exchange set the tone for the game. Sometimes it worked out that way. Every ball thrown landed perfectly in Nate's arms and every route he ran was precise. His focus seemed to be hyper-acute, and he could see clear lanes every time he ran, jigging the grasp of tackles and breaking free for extra yardage when they managed to get a hold of him. My-name-is-not-Mac caught up to him more than once but he'd made two touchdowns and his team was up by seven going into the half. Now with time winding down and coming out of the huddle for what was likely the last play, he mentally prepared himself.

He ran his route and turned back for the ball. His eyes followed it out of its arc. The ball fell perfectly into his arms. Pivoting, he ran with all his might for the goal line. Someone grabbed at his waist, but he spun away and kept running. A defender hit him hard from the side and sent him sprawling. When he finished rolling, he realized he had landed in the end zone.

Green and black jerseys rushed him in congratulations with pats on the helmet, chest, and back. He turned toward the crowd searching for his dad. David was on his feet clapping and whistling. Nate's heart swelled.

Then, behind his dad, he saw the kids. His touch-down-scoring-high dropped like a dead man's blood pressure. Their eyes were dark pools against their pale skin. The older one lifted his arm and silently pointed at Nate making the hair on the back of his neck tingle. Then as quick as they were there, they were gone.

He dropped his gaze to the cheerleaders, hoping Sophia had seen them, too. He had to know he wasn't going crazy.

The cheerleaders were making a human pyramid in celebration. Missy, as the flyer, was perched on one foot on the outstretched hands of two girls who were standing on the shoulders of two other girls. Her back arched, she reached behind to pull her free foot towards the back of her head into a position called a scorpion. He only knew because Missy told him the day before about her stunt.

Suddenly, her smiling face contorted into a horrified expression. She lost her balance and kicked her free foot forward. The momentum threw her backward. She dropped, missing both spotters and landing flat on her back. A small cloud of dust swirled under the impact. The crowd gasped.

The next thing Nate knew he was running all out toward her.

\*\*\*

Nate's head hung low as if the weight of the past couple of hours had crushed the back of his neck. Everything felt fuzzy, and he kept replaying it in his head to get it straight. He ran to Missy. She wasn't moving, her eyes shut. Call 911, someone yelled. He took off his helmet but couldn't remember what he had done with it. A trickle of blood stained the corner of her mouth. Kneeling next to her he wiped it away with the back of his hand. The next thing he remembered was seeing his dad crouched beside her. You're OK, baby, he said. But clearly, she wasn't.

He wasn't sure how he had ended up in the back seat of Mr. Lewis' little car. Sophia sat in the front seat and cried all the way to the hospital. Her dad rested his hand on her knee and kept patting it but not talking.

They had been in the waiting area of the emergency room for what felt like days, but he knew it couldn't have been that long. The chairs were stiff and unforgiving. They seemed to commiserate with his tension. David sat next to him in the same slouched way and gripped the armrest of the chair as if he thought he might slip out of it and pool on the floor. Mel sat across from them and she stared at a point on the floor with glassy eyes. Her hair, usually held in a sleek style, was a disordered mop of frizz. She tried to tuck it behind her ears, but it wasn't helping. Dark eye makeup smeared around her eyes making her look even more worn out.

Nate's thoughts drifted to Sophia. She had looked like that then magically, two minutes of makeup, and ta-dah. Like nothing had ever happened. Too bad there wasn't any makeup that could be smeared on life.

Sophia hadn't looked up or said a word since they sat down in the narrow white room. All of her magic makeup smeared away. She was still wearing her cheer uniform, but it had lost its crispness. He'd dumped his shoulder pads somewhere between the arrival of the ambulance and getting in Mr. Lewis' car. But like his helmet, he had no idea where they were. He wore a sweat and grass stained tee shirt, football pants, and cleats. It must not have been hard for people who saw them to know a game had gone terribly wrong.

Mr. Lewis came into the room with a drink carrier and tray.

"I brought coffee and some snacks," he said. "The cafeteria had some good stuff."

Mel reached for a coffee.

"Thanks," David said, but he didn't reach for anything.

Nate feared his voice wouldn't work, so he shook his head. He cracked his knuckles. Mel gave him a look.

"Any word?" Mr. Lewis asked.

"No, nothing yet," Mel said. To Sophia she said, "Eat something, honey. You must be hungry."

Sophia took a cinnamon roll and held it lightly in both hands. Her eyes were shiny with tears.

"I'm so sorry, Mrs. Camden. We practiced those stunts, we had it down. I, I just don't know what happened."

Mel took Sophia's hands in her own, "It was an accident. You have nothing to be sorry for."

They waited in silence.

"We should head out, honey," Mr. Lewis said to Sophia. "The Camdens can let us know when there is some news."

"Of course, we'll call. Thanks for bringing Nate over, Rick," Mel said.

"Oh sure, no problem. I can help David get his car tomorrow from the school if you need me to."

"Oh! Yeah, I didn't even think of that since I rode with Missy. That would be great. I'll call you in the morning?" David asked.

"Sounds good. Try not to worry. These things can look worse than they actually are." Rick put a protective arm around Sophia and escorted her out.

The three of them sat motionless and wordless after they left. It was as if collectively they knew that if they moved or made a sound bad news would be able to find them.

A small man in a white coat bustled into the room, "Mr. and Mrs. Camden?"

His parents jumped to their feet and answered in a united, "Yes."

"Please, sit down," he said taking the chair Sophia had vacated.

"Is she OK?" Mel asked.

"She will be fine."

Mel's posture crumbled as if the news had melted the last of her stamina.

"Sorry it took so long to get back out here to you. We are little short-handed tonight. We found that the skull is not fractured, but she does have a concussion and a hematoma on the back of her head that will last a few days. Ice and rest will do the trick. She hit her mouth, likely on the head of another girl, pretty common injury in her sport. Her lip is swollen, but she only needed a couple stitches. However, because of the way she fell she has a grade three AC separation in her shoulder."

"What does that mean?" David asked.

"It means that there is a complete tear of the AC ligament and the coracoclavicular ligaments in her shoulder. There are no broken bones, but she is possibly going to need surgery to repair the ligaments. I want to keep her overnight to have the orthopedic department look at her in the morning but also because she lost consciousness after she hit her head."

Nate's heart dropped. "She can't stay here by herself," he blurted.

"Of course not. I'll stay with her," said Mel. "Can you run home and grab me a few things, David?"

"Yeah, sure."

"She's groggy from the pain medication we gave her for the shoulder, but you're welcome to stay with her. You can go in and see her now if you'd like."

The hospital room was tranquil and still. A light on the wall above the bed cast a greenish sheen. There was a bed on the other side of her, but it was empty. Missy looked elfish in the bed. Her curly hair had taken on a life of its own as if running from the bump on the back of her head. Her bottom lip looked like a plastic surgery gone wrong and her arm rested in a sling. She tried to smile at them.

"Way to go for my first cheer performance," she mumbled through the fat lip.

"Thank God you're OK," Mel said.

After they sat with her for a while, Mel decided that she needed to go home and get her things. It would be easier than trying to tell David where everything she needed was. David walked her out to the car, leaving Missy and Nate alone.

"Nate, grab my cell phone," she said.

"What do you need your phone for, Missy? You can hardly talk."

"Texting. Pleeeeease," she pleaded.

She looked so pathetic he couldn't turn her down. He rummaged through a white plastic bag in the cupboard next to her bed. The phone was buried under her rumpled cheer uniform. The screen was blank and it didn't respond when he punched the button.

"Sorry, it's dead."

"Oh God! Seriously? I have to know what everyone is saying. I'm so embarrassed."

"Embarrassed?"

"God, Nate, I just fell on my ass in front of the whole school!"

"Technically it was your back and who cares what they say."

"I do," she whimpered. "My head hurts and my shoulder is killer. Nate, they say I'll be out for six weeks. They'll replace me on the squad." Her eyes shimmered.

"You'll be fine. You'll be cheering again by the time basketball starts up. What happened?"

She cried quietly. "I was so happy. You were playing so great. I thought I saw something weird, in the crowd, by dad. I got freaked out and lost my concentration. And my balance."

"What did you see?"

"You'll think I'm crazy or something, or it's because I hit my head."

"No, I won't think you're crazy. I thought I saw something weird too, right before you fell."

"What did you see?"

"I don't know. Some weird kids. A ghost, maybe," he shrugged.

Her eyes widened. "Nate, that's what I saw. Two ghost kids and one pointed at me and then they disappeared."

"That's funny, I thought they were pointing at me."

She gawked. "What the -"

"I don't know."

"Nate, I'm scared."

"Don't be scared. Maybe it's some kind of a prank or something. I don't think they would actually try to hurt anyone. It was just an accident."

It all sounded good but tasted like lies.

## CHAPTER TEN

Linda's head was killing her. The best sleep she had gotten the night before was the hour after she turned off her alarm. Now she was running late, and Mrs. Snyder had to cover her morning duty. Mr. Greene was already in a foul mood because of the construction accident, the lockdown, and then there had been a terrible accident at the football game the night before. He had sent out a group text last night to warn staff not to discuss the topics of his displeasure with students to avoid undue excitement. Translation, he wanted to avoid responsibility in case of any pending lawsuits or other trouble.

"Mrs. Snyder, thank you so much. I'm here now," Linda said after she waded through a sea of kids to get to a slight woman in tweed skirt and jacket.

Mrs. Snyder's white hair was pulled tightly back into a severe bun making her eyes look slightly catlike. "That's fine, dear. You'll owe me one."

"Yes, of course!"

"Umm, Miss Garza?"

She looked behind her to see a wiry boy with a ball cap on backward. She didn't know his name.

"Good morning," she said.

"I think maybe, there might be, a fight down there," he said.

"A fight? Down where?"

He pointed toward the sidewalk. Sure enough, there was a large group of girls standing in a tight circle. More kids were streaming that way. Linda hurried to the group and pushed her way through to the two girls in the middle of the throng.

"What is going on here?"

Neither girl answered.

"Kimberli and Sophia, what is the problem," she said evenly.

"Nothing is, like, wrong. We were just discussing what happened to Missy," Kimberli said.

Sophia dropped her eyes. "It's fine."

"No! It is not fine!" Kimberli shouted.

"Hey, ladies! I know we are all upset about Missy's accident."

"It wasn't an accident! She just wanted to like hang on Missy's brother. She distracted Missy on purpose!"

Sophia's head popped up. "What are you talking about? Me and Missy are friends. It was my dad's idea to give him a ride to the hospital. I would never hurt Missy on purpose!"

"As if anyone here believes that. We all saw you dragging him around the other morning to do God-knows-what off campus."

"Oh my God. You are such a jealous psycho." She felt her social standing flush out of her heart.

"You little b-" She reached out to grab Sophia.

Linda pushed them apart with her outstretched arms, "Girls! That is it! Get yourselves to the office right now! The rest of you move on right now unless you wish to have detention!"

Another teacher helped Linda escort the girls to the office. Kimberli was put in Mr. Greene's office and Sophia was ushered into a vacant conference room. She had never been in trouble at school before.

Linda came in and sat down next to her. "So, what happened?"

Sophia shrugged.

"Hmm. It sounded like a fight over a boy."

Sophia rolled her eyes. "Maybe for Kimberli."

"Listen, boys come and go but friends, that's what's important."

"Kimberli isn't really my friend."

"You guys are always together."

"Just because of cheerleading. Outside of school, we don't even really talk or anything." Sophia's eyes looked so sad. It reminded Linda of a former student and her heart pinched.

Beat up Chuck Taylors suspended in the middle of a small dark room entered Linda's mind. She felt bile rise in her throat.

The door swung open with a scrape, and Mr. Greene ushered Kimberli in, saving Linda from the memory. "I understand how upset you girls are over Missy's mishap but pointing fingers and placing blame won't help. Cheerleading is a dangerous sport and sometimes girls get hurt."

Both girls shook their heads in agreement.

"Kimberli, as the captain of the team it's your job to set the decorum of teamwork, even in adversity."

"I know, Mr. Greene. I'm just like so emotional over Missy's accident. I'm really sorry I let it get to me like that."

"OK. Well for the sake of the team-"

"Squad," Kimberli interrupted.

"Fine, squad, I need you two to make up."

"I'm so sorry I like took this all out on you, Sophia. I know how hard you worked with Missy."

"It's OK."

Kimberli leaned down and hugged Sophia. Mr. Greene and Linda looked on with pleased smiles.

"Excellent. I knew you could be reasonable young ladies. Now you girls get off to class," Mr. Greene said.

Sophia followed Kimberli out of the room.

"I'm so glad that worked out," she heard Linda say.

She rolled her eyes at Kimberli's back. Being suspended would have been better. Adults were so clueless. Hugs or no hugs it would be war. Just as messy and devastating as any armed conflict in its own way. When Kimberli tugged hard at the little hairs at the back of her neck as she hugged her, Sophia knew it was on.

By lunchtime, word of the fight had gotten around. When Sophia entered the lunchroom heads turned to look at her and she could hear the swish of swirling whispers. Her usual lunch crowd of fellow cheerleaders was sitting at the round table in the center of the room where they always sat. In the Kimberli mandated quest for thigh-gaps, there wasn't a spec of food on the table. The girls at the table turned to look at her and then bent their heads together. Something was whispered, and they all laughed.

Sophia hugged herself and scanned the room for an open spot or better yet an escape route. She decided to eat her meager lunch of yogurt in the girl's bathroom and made her way there. If nobody noticed her go in she could stay until lunch was over. Eyes glued to the target, she moved through the crowd. A hand grabbed her arm and she jumped, ready for battle.

"Wanna seat?" Garrett motioned to the spot next to him.

She looked up and down the table of 80s rock band t-shirts. Three longboards laid on the table like centerpieces. None of the expressions were welcoming.

"No, I'm good," she mumbled and continued her quest.

"What the frig, man?" a boy with shoulder-length hair the color of cherry Kool-Aid said.

"What? The girl needed a place to sit," Garrett said.

"You're lucky we let you sit here, poser," the boy said, and the others laughed.

"Shut up," Garrett said as he threw a potato chip.

Sophia let the restroom door bang shut behind her. She locked herself in the farthest stall, relieved that the rest were empty. Leaning her head against the cold steel of the door she squeezed her eyes tight against the tears that burned behind her lids. She hugged herself with one arm letting her fingers put pressure on the fresh cuts she had made the night before. She pushed herself back from the door, took a deep breath, and opened her eyes.

*Sophia Lewis is a crack whore*, was scratched into the door.

Turning, she pressed her back against the cold steel door. She felt in her pocket for the paperclip she had slipped in there earlier. Her fingers trembled as she pulled and twisted it straight.

She hesitated, telling herself the lie, thinking she should use it to scratch out the graffiti. Instead, she plunged the end of the clip as deep as she dared into the bony area between her breasts. Twisting she made the hole a little bigger. Not too much, just enough to trade the emotional pain for physical pain. The tension in her body trickled away with the slight flow of bright red blood.

# CHAPTER ELEVEN

Inna hadn't shown up for school and had broken the most sacred rule of teaching. She hadn't called for a sub.

It clearly pushed Mr. Greene over the edge he was forever perched on, and he took it out on the whole staff with several nasty emails over the course of the day. Linda could only imagine what Inna's inbox looked like.

She tried calling Inna and texting her at various times throughout the day, but the messages and calls went unanswered. Now Linda sat undecided in the grocery store parking lot tapping the wheel of her VW bug. She dug her cell phone out of her purse and tried Inna's cell one more time. No answer. Without leaving a message, she stabbed end on the phone and started the car.

Inna's house was a modest ranch just west of Dark Pine Hills in an area called Rocky Meadows. The house sat at the end of a street that dead-ended in a wooded open space that was just beginning to come alive with fall colors. Though small, the front yard was carefully maintained, and the porch was neatly arranged with potted plants. There were no cars parked in front on the street and the driveway stood empty. The plantation shutters were securely shut in every window.

As Linda approached the front door she felt uneasy and inexplicably isolated. The whole neighborhood was dead silent, not even a bird was chirping or a dog barking. She rang the bell and waited. No movement, so she rang again, holding it longer. Still nothing.

It was starting to look like no one was home. Linda shifted her feet getting ready to leave when she realized that small seeds had been spilled across the porch in front of the door. Leaning over, she could see they were poppy seeds. The door sucked open, startling her.

"Inna?" she asked to the dark crack.

"Linda? What are you doing here?"

"You haven't been answering my calls. I got worried, so here I am."

"I'm sick."

"I figured. You didn't even call for a sub. Are you OK?"

"Yeah, I'm just not feeling well."

"Can I come in?"

Silence.

"Inna? I'm not leaving here until I can lay my eyes on you."

The door crept open and Linda slipped in. The house was dark and airless. Inna stood back from the door wrapped tightly in a bulky flowered robe that reached to the floor. Her face was gaunt and pale. Sections of her auburn hair were poking out in dangerous spikes from the loose bun at the back of her head.

"Do you have the flu?"

"I don't know. I just feel like crap."

Linda tossed her handbag on the dark hardwood floor and reached out to touch Inna's face. She could feel the heat coming off her body before she even touched her skin.

"You're running a fever."

"You think? I'm, I'm freezing."

"Where's your husband?"

"Ben? He's been out of town at a convention." Inna shuffled into the family room and sprawled on the couch.

"Have you eaten anything?" Linda asked.

"No, I don't think I could keep anything down."

"Let's at least try some tea and toast," Linda said as she headed for the kitchen.

She returned moments later to find Inna sound asleep. Linda set the steaming mug of weak tea and plate of dry toast on the large center ottoman of the chocolate brown leather sectional. Inna's chest heaved and Linda could hear a deep wheezing from her lungs. Thoughts of pneumonia crossed her mind. Then Inna stopped breathing; panic flooded Linda's chest. Without warning, Inna sat bolt upright, arms flailing and eyes bulging.

"What was that?" she shouted.

"What was what?" Linda replied startled.

"That knocking!" Inna's eyes were wild.

"There is no knocking. I think you were dreaming," Linda said, and she tried to catch Inna's arms.

Inna's brows crunched together and her dry, cracked lips pursed in an attempt to keep from crying.

"Have you seen a doctor? You're scaring me."

Inna shook her head and the tears won. Linda dropped her wrists and hugged her. Inna rocked with hoarse weeping for several moments. Linda's concern was growing with each passing moment.

"Oh my God, Inna. What is it?"

"Linda, I think I'm having a breakdown of some sort!"

"What? What do you mean? You're just sick."

"I- I'm seeing things. Hearing things."

"What kind of things?" It had to be the fever.

"I don't- I don't know. Nightmares when I'm awake, ghosts, fairy tales, I don't know!"

Linda listened carefully as Inna recalled the incident with the mysterious boys at the school.

"Kids messing around. The eyes could have been a trick of the light because your eyes were tired from looking at the computer," Linda said.

"I know that makes sense, but the feeling they gave me, Linda. It was something else. Then there was what happened after I got home."

"What happened?"

"When I first got home, I got sick, so I was going to go to bed. I was just about to lie down when I heard someone at the front door. I thought it was Ben coming home early, but when I opened the door, they were there."

"Those same kids?"

Inna's voice had taken on a strange tone and she stared off into the distance, "The same kids from school. They told me I had to let them in. That what they wanted wouldn't take long."

"What? Did you let them in? You should have called the police! Did they hurt you?" Linda jumped up as if to take action.

Inna only shook her head slowly, "No. I didn't let them in, I slammed the door shut, but they kept knocking and knocking on the door and windows. I hid in my closet until they finally left me alone."

"Oh my God, Inna! They must be high on drugs. Trying to rob you, maybe. We should call the police now."

Inna dragged her eyes to Linda's. "When I was little my Russian grandma would tell us stories about vampires. When I saw those kids, that's what I thought of."

"What do you mean?"

"Not Bela Lugosi type vampires but the Eretich, I think she called them. They were people who practiced witchcraft and sold their souls to the devil. After they died, they would rise from the dead and pass for normal people, for the most part." Her words were breathy.

"Inna, that has nothing to do with what is happening."

"The only thing these Eretich do is try to turn people from their faith. If you saw an Eretich's real eyes it would cause a slow withering death." She looked wide-eyed at Linda. "I know how this sounds, but it explains why I'm sick. I saw their eyes. I know they aren't human."

"Inna, I-"

Linda was cut short by the sound of the front door knob jiggling. Inna's eyes grew wider and she clutched Linda's arm. They both gasped as the front door flung open.

"Inna? I'm home!" Ben swept into the room with his luggage still in hand. He froze when he saw the scene of the women clutching each other. "Are you guys, OK?"

"Ben! Ben, this is Linda from school."

"Nice to meet you," Ben said looking around the room as if an explanation for the strange scene could be found.

"You too. Look, Inna is very sick and I just came by to check on her."

"Not feeling well, honey?"

"I thought I- No, I don't feel well," Inna mumbled.

"I think she needs to see a doctor. She has a fever and is very upset," Linda said.

"OK. Honey, do you think you need a doctor?"

Inna retched down the front of her robe, splashing the carpet.

"I think that's a yes," Linda said.

After Ben and Inna went back to an exam room in the ER Linda went to find a restroom to clean herself up. She had ridden with Inna in the backseat and the large mixing bowl they had brought along proved to be inadequate for the job. The light blue blouse she was wearing was a total loss. A very sweet nurse had given her a blue scrub shirt to replace it.

She had washed her hands vigorously. She cared deeply for Inna, but whatever Inna had, she didn't want it. When she had scrubbed up as best she could in the tiny restroom she headed back to the ER to wait for Inna and Ben. The glow of a vending machine lured her on a slight detour; her stomach needed some carbonization. A young boy bent over with his arm inside the slot of the snack machine fishing for the treat he had purchased. Familiarity touched her.

"Nate?"

He looked up at her, his dark wavy hair falling into his eyes. "Oh, hi Miss. What are you doing here? Are you a nurse at night or something?"

She looked down at her top, "Oh! No, I'm here with a friend. Are you here with your sister?"

"Yeah. She is going to have surgery on her shoulder."

"I'm sorry to hear that. We hoped it wasn't serious."

Nate shrugged. "It's not, really. I guess they have to fix a tendon or something. Doctor says she'll be fine."

"That's good. Will I see you in class tomorrow?"

"I guess it depends on when they schedule Missy's surgery."

"OK. Well, I hope everything works out."

"Thanks, I hope your friend will be all right."

"I'm sure she will. Thanks," she said.

Nate turned away and took his phone out and turned it on for the first time today. Everyone had been blowing it up with texts. There had been some kind of fight between Sophia and Kimberli, and it was over him!

One of the texts came from Kimberli. How did she get his number?

*Kimberli: Hi Nate. How's missy?*

His thumb wavered over the screen.

*Kimberli: If you r going to miss school again I could get your homework and drop it by your house if u want.*

Another text chimed in almost on top of that one.

*Garrett: Dude, Kim lifted my phone and got your number. Sorry*

*Nate: Wondered how she got it. Are you with her?*

*Garrett: Not now. I was at her house earlier*

*Nate: ? Don't worry about it. She just wants to know about Missy*

*Garrett: Im friends with her sister*

*Nate: She has a sister? Poor girl*

*Garrett: LOL Hows missy?*

*Nate: She's going to be OK. What's this about a fight?*

*Garrett: Not really a fight. Just yelling. Mostly about you.*

*Nate: WTH*

*Garrett: IDK but it almost went to blows*

*Nate: Call me. Something to tell you. Too long for text*

*Kimberli: Text me back to let me know if you want me bring your homework or whatever*

*Kimberli: I hope she's ok. Are you ok? Do you need someone to talk to?*

*Kimberli: Text me!*

Nate slipped his phone back into his pocket. He was way too tired to text Kimberli back. Besides, he wanted to hear Sophia's side to the story. He found a bench and sat down to wait for Garrett's call.

"Sorry about that. My mom needed something real quick." It had taken Garrett a few minutes to get back to him.

"Something weird happened," Nate said.

"What?"

"I saw those weird kids at the football game, in the stands. Missy says she saw them too and that's what made her lose her balance. This is gonna sound weird, but, well, their eyes were totally black and we both saw them disappear into thin air."

"What? Seriously?"

"I don't know what to think. Either we are being seriously punked or, or, I don't know what."

"Haunted?" Garrett offered.

"Yeah. Maybe."

"Dude, that's crazy. Not that you're crazy! I totally believe in that stuff. I knew there was something wrong with the kid I talked to. I mean more than he was just a weird kid."

"Really?"

"Yeah. I felt sick after I got away from him. Like something in me knew it was evil."

"Well, what should we do?"

"I don't know. Let me do some research."

"OK, but nothing like calling a ghost hunter show." Nate knew if his image was splashed across the screen for an episode of Ghost Wranglers, or something like that, he could kiss a career with the Navy SEALs goodbye.

Silence.

"Garrett?"

"Well, I'll let you know what I find out, OK?"

"All right. Was Sophia OK after the fight today?"

"I don't know. I've been trying to text her."

"You have her number?" There was a hint of disbelief.

"Yeah. I asked her for it in class. She looked like she needed a friend."

"Yeah. She probably does."

# CHAPTER TWELVE

Garrett put his phone down and unburied his laptop. He hadn't used it all summer and now couldn't remember his password. He'd only set one because Haley messed around on it one day and totally jacked it up. *Oh yeah.*

He typed: *Hal3yisaBra7* and his machine bloomed to life. Ordinarily, he would have just used his phone, but he needed more firepower for this. He launched the web browser and waited for all his security measures to boot.

Nate didn't want him to, but he searched for some of the ghost hunter shows he had seen on TV. Then he searched for parapsychology, creepy kids, and finally, what can I do if I am being haunted. None of those brought him satisfying answers, although he thought a television show would be sort of cool.

With a few more clicks, a page with a black background and animated burning flames across the header filled the screen. The title, The Witch's Pyre, flashed from red to yellow to orange and back again. He could have texted, but seeing the website gave him a vague feeling of security. He clicked on a message box.

*Hey it's G. We need to talk.* He hit send.

He waited, but he knew he probably wouldn't get a reply right away. That was fine with him. He needed time to figure out how to discuss the situation.

On a whim, he went to what he liked to think of as a Dark Net site. It wasn't that nefarious, but it was a hidden page. It was his school's confessions page. He didn't know who set it up, but a kid in the computer lab told him about it. Most of it was boring things about who liked whom and who went all the way and with said whom. Sometimes it was complaints about teachers, mostly Mr. Greene. Once in a while, a house party was announced, but that's not what he was looking for. Maybe others had seen the same weird kids and posted it as a Creepypasta or something.

Garrett scrolled through the posts. None of them were what he anticipated finding. His disapproval grew with each screen. He looked over to his phone and considered it. He wiped his sweaty hands on his pants leg and made the call. It rang twice, and he was about to disconnect when the other end connected.

"Hello?"

"Sophia?" Lame. Of course it was her.

"Yeah?" Her voice dripped with suspicion.

"It's Garrett."

"Oh. Hey." Relief flooded her voice.

"I just talked to Nate. Missy is gonna be fine."

"Yeah, I know. My dad talked to her mom."

"Oh."

Silence.

"Nate said that Missy fell because she saw those kids in the stands," he blurted.

"You mean, *the kids*?"

"Yeah. She saw them and so did Nate. Nate said they had black eyes and disappeared. It scared Missy so much she fell."

Silence.

"I don't think it's kids punking us. I have a friend who knows a lot about this stuff. We're going to ask her what she thinks."

"Yeah, OK. But Garrett..."

"Yeah?"

"Can you leave my name out of it? I have enough trouble right now."

"Sure." He hesitated. "I can do that. Have you seen the confessions page?"

"The what?"

"You know, it's a page where people from our school post secret crushes or whatever."

"I didn't know we had one."

"Well, we do. Maybe you should check it out. There's a hidden link to it from the school website. Just click the "I" in hills."

They listened to each other breathe.

"You know Nate doesn't even like Kimberli."

"I don't like him either! I mean, I like him, but not like that," she said.

Garrett smiled into the empty room. A feeling of protectiveness toward her flooded him. "Hey, sorry. I gotta go. My mom is calling me. Try not to worry about all the drama."

"OK, thanks."

Sophia ended the call and pulled up the school website and clicked the hidden link. She felt like the breath had been knocked out of her. A page of posts came up and her name was all over the place. Anonymous users were posting everything from how Sophia was too skinny to how her long hair had to be fake extensions.

Just when she thought it couldn't get much worse, she scrolled down to find someone had attached a picture to their post. Despite her better judgment, she clicked it. A photo of her at cheer practice just having finished a tumbling run filled the screen. Her arms were over her head and just barely peeking out from under her top an angry red slice in her skin was visible.

The caption read: *Mental case cutter. Put yourself out of our misery. Cuts go on the wrists honey.*

Right under that, the first comment read: *Jealous much? Whoever posted this is the mental case beeyotch!*

Despite the tears welling in her eyes, she smiled and whispered, "Thanks, Garrett."

She read a few more posts, each one more vile than the first. Sophia dropped her phone to the floor and threw herself onto the bed. Tears flooded down the sides of her head, rushing past her temples and soaking her hair. Pressing her fists hard into her eyes, she rolled onto her stomach; she buried her face in the worn soft lavender comforter. She couldn't count how many times her tears had soaked this blanket.

She lay like that for several minutes. Her fingers absently worked into one of the many small tears in the fabric, caressing the rough batting below. The calming sensation took over and her tears slowed to a trickle. She sat up on the edge of the bed, looking for the box of tissues she knew was there somewhere.

It shouldn't be too hard to find. Her bedroom was practically empty. The twin bed, the matching dresser and a night table, a few books, posters, and that was it. The same furniture she'd since she was about nine years old. That was the same year It had happened. It had caused so many parts of her life to stall. She and her dad had tried to move forward, but It just kept dragging them back.

Her mind went back to It. She felt helpless to keep the thoughts out like a leak that had sprung on the roof and no one had a ladder to climb up and fix it. Even though she replayed the memories over and over, they came in flashes now instead of detail. It always started with the cop at their front door, the way his eyes looked when he saw her.

"There's been an accident," he said.

The next flash was the hospital.

"You're too little to go in, honey. But if you stand on this chair you can see your mommy. She's going to be fine," someone said.

She pressed her nose to the glass. It was cold. Her mother was in the bed with tubes going every which way and machines flashing and beeping around her. Her face swollen in hues of purple, blue, and green. She watched her dad go in. His knees buckled and the nurse behind him helped him to a chair.

The next flash was the tow yard.

She held her dad's hand. The day was crisp and her thin jacket wasn't enough to keep her from shivering. The air smelled of old grease and dust. The gravel crunched beneath their feet like dry bones as they walked among the metal corpses.

"You can see the insurance company is gonna have to total it," a man in greasy coveralls walking with them said.

It didn't look like a car. Crumbled and bent in impossible ways, some of the familiar blue paint still clung to twisted metal here and there. Traces of blood on the shards of the destroyed windshield. It was hard to imagine her mother's body twisted and broken in there.

The next scene was at their house in Arvada, a suburb north of Denver. A little clapboard house painted yellow. A flash of her mom using the walker to get inside.

"Hi, baby. Get my pills from the car, would you? I'm going to need some medicine after the ride home," she said to Sophia.

Medicine.

No one noticed that it had become a problem until things started disappearing from their home. That included the grocery money and eventually matured into anything not nailed down. When Sophia came home to discover that all of her dance medals from competitions were pawned, they should have realized how bad it had gotten. Maybe it was naiveté, maybe it was flat out denial, but they didn't. It wasn't until her mom was arrested for stealing a prescription pad from a doctor's office that they had no choice but to face the reality.

What her mom hadn't used to pay for pills Rick spent sending her to various rehab stints, and for lawyers. Sophia had to give up dancing because they couldn't afford it with all the other expenses.

At first, judges had been lenient and facilitated treatment, but finally the mercy ran out. Sophia's mom went to jail for probation violation for the first time when Sophia was twelve. From there it was a revolving door of jail, rehab, stealing, and who knew what else. Sophia wasn't a baby and she knew what people sometimes did to get drugs.

Sophia found a private ballet boarding school online and secretly sent an application. Using her very best handwriting, she filled out the dance resume of where she had studied, awards and competitions she had won. Sneaking to her old dance studio, she begged the instructor to write a letter on her behalf. She created the audition tape in her basement with a cell phone propped up on books. If she could get a scholarship, she could live there and dance. There would be no worry of her mom stealing from her. There would be a chance at a normal life. She didn't want to abandon her dad, but she had to get out of the situation. Even at her young age she knew it would only get worse.

One afternoon, her dad met her at the door with a light pink envelope with the ballet school's emblem on the back flap. At first, her heart had leaped, had she gotten in? Was her dad angry? But then she saw the look on his face. He looked like the weight of life had pulled his skin down.

"Honey, I'm sorry," his voice strangled.

She took the envelope, the top seam a jagged opening. She pulled the single sheet of matching pink paper out and unfolded it.

*We appreciate the time it took to send us your materials, but we find that the inconsistencies in training make it impossible for us to extend an invitation for you to attend our schoo*l. It had been signed, *yours in dance*.

She soaked her bed with tears. Her dad sat quietly stroking her hair.

That seemed to be the last straw for Rick. They sold their house and most of their furniture and bought this house on foreclosure. They might not be able to afford to furnish it but he was determined to get her into a good neighborhood and good school district as far away from the memories as they could afford to go.

One of the first things he had done when they got settled was sign her up for dance school. She knew it was expensive and she loved him for it. He worked two jobs to pay for everything, including the lingering bills from her mom. He worked as a help-desk technician for a financial firm during the day and at an electronics store at night and most weekends. Some nights, like tonight, she would give up all of it to have him around more.

She felt a pressure building in her chest.

A loud scraping noise from outside startled her out of her thoughts. She went to her bedroom window and moved the lavender sheet hung as a curtain out of the way. The garage was set back from the front of the house where her bedroom was but she could see shadows moving on the driveway.

She dropped the makeshift curtain and tiptoed down the stairs, through the house into the kitchen, and pressed her ear to the door that led to the garage. Not hearing anything, she pushed the door open and peered into the darkened interior.

Something banged on the outside of the garage door making it sway in its tracks. She heard laughing. Creepy boys who would want to come in crossed her mind.

"Come on! Hurry, I think someone's home!" a girl's voice came from the other side of the door.

Sophia stood motionless for a few moments. When all was quiet and still, she snuck through the garage to the side door. Inching the door open, she peered around the wall of the garage. No one in sight. She walked out onto the driveway and looked up and down the empty street. Sophia turned back to the garage to go inside.

Scrawled across the length of the garage door, in hot pink letters, S-L-U-T.

Shock and embarrassment began a low boil in her stomach. Her head swiveled checking for witnesses. She rushed to the door and scratched at the S with her fingernail. The color flaked off in dusty pieces. Thank God, it was only sidewalk paint. She could have it washed off in plenty of time before her dad got home.

She swirled the paint flecks with her thumb on the tip of her index finger. The pink flakes stained her skin a cheerful blush color. A mental picture of the letters on the door carved deeply into her skin made her gasp. She had never tried that before, and she wondered what relief that would bring.

# CHAPTER THIRTEEN

Nate was relieved when Garrett told him that he found somebody to answer their questions about the strange events. They made a plan to meet up at Garrett's after Nate got done with football practice. He followed the same path as the day he came to Garrett's to swim. No music blaring this time. Nate almost backpedaled when he saw Lindsey in the pool chair next to Garrett. No way was he going to talk about this weirdness in front of her. He walked warily to an empty chair, putting Garrett between them.

"Hey," Garrett said.

"Hey." Nate couldn't keep the unease out of his voice.

Garrett said, "It's cool. Lindsey is part of the research. I would have left her out of it if there was any other way."

"Does she know?" Nate felt sick.

"Uh, hey guys, I'm right here," Lindsey said.

"Sorry, Lindsey. It's just..."

"Look guys, I'm not here to judge. Garrett said that you guys had a weird experience and need help figuring it out."

"Yeah, but I meant like professional." Nate eyed Garrett.

Garrett handed him his phone. The browser was open to the Witch's Pyre web page. Nate scrolled the authoritative blog posts about the paranormal. Why hadn't he thought to check this before? Garrett and Sophia had mentioned it when they walked back to school from the store.

He googled it yesterday. Everyone from ghost shows to the nightly news wanted to interview the author, but no one knew who wrote it. That sparked rumors that it was written either by a celebrity, a well-known scientist, or a ghost. Then it dawned on him.

"Wait. Lindsey Pyre. You are Witch's Pyre?"

"The one and only," she said.

"Holy shit!" Nate was impressed.

"Right?" Garrett said.

"OK. So she's an expert."

"That I am boys," she smiled.

"I thought maybe Sophia would be here, too," Nate said.

"I've been trying to call and text her, but no answer and all I get is voice mail. She's a no-show at school," Garrett said.

"She probably didn't want to face the cheer coven after all the crap they posted about her online," Lindsey said.

"Um, my sister is a cheerleader."

Lindsey shrugged. "She's new. They haven't destroyed her innocence yet, but they will. I should know. The head witch is my sister. I know, it's an insult to witches everywhere."

"You're Kimberli's sister?" Nate arched his eyebrows.

"Well, Kimberli-with-two-i's is technically my stepsister. I got an awesome stepmom in the deal. But, please, enough about her and 'as the cheers turn'. Tell me what happened to you guys."

Garrett related everything that had happened up to now. Nate squirmed in his seat and threw in here and there. Lindsey moved to sit on the pool deck in front of Nate and listened without making any comment.

"What the hell. That's freaking creepy," she said at the end of the telling.

"Well, thanks Captain Obvious. What should we do?" Garrett asked.

The French doors facing the pool popped open with a loud bang and they shifted their attention. Haley bounded out the door and bounced her curly head toward them.

"Garrett, play with me!" she squealed and she jumped into his lap.

He let out a groan and breath all in one, "Not now, Haley! Can't you see I'm busy?"

"Lindsey!" she shrieked and jumped on her.

"Hey, Haley," Lindsey said.

Haley turned to take in Nate. She pushed her soft dark blonde curls out of her face.

"Hi Haley," he said.

She smiled a smile that put the sun to shame.

"Get outta here you little nut! Mom! Get Haley!"

She giggled. "I'll leave if you play with me later."

"OK, all right! Now get lost."

She bounced back through the door the same way she bounced out.

"Sorry about that. OK, Lindsey, what do we do?" Garrett asked.

"Well, I hate to admit this, but I don't know."

"Come on, Lindsey! What the hell?" Garrett said.

"Calm down, give me a minute." She rummaged through the bag that sat next to her chair and pulled out a tablet computer. Her hands flew over the surface, and she turned it around for them to see.

A web site called Black Eyed Kids was on the screen.

"That's it!" Garrett shouted.

"It's run by a reporter who had a similar encounter as you guys. There are reports about these kids all over the world. They call them B-E-Ks for short."

Nate and Garrett scanned the site. The encounters sounded very similar to what had happened to them.

"People as far away as Germany? A US Marine in his barracks?" Nate said.

"I know, right?"

"So what do we do about it?" Garrett asked.

"Well, I don't know of any reports of several people seeing them, or seeing them repeatedly. Even the reporter never saw them again and his deal was way back in 1996. I might know someone who could help us."

"Great. When could we talk to them?" Nate asked.

Lindsey shrugged. "Right now."

Nate wasn't thrilled to find out the source of information was 30 miles away in downtown Denver. He was even less thrilled when Lindsey announced they would ride the bus there. He was ready to forget it when she told them they had to cut through the woods to get to the nearest bus stop.

"I don't know about this, guys," he said.

"It's fine. I do this all the time." Lindsey said. She swapped her flip flops for running shoes that she got from Garrett's house. The idea that she kept clothes at Garrett's house created a small knot under Nate's sternum.

Garrett shrugged one shoulder. "Ok, I'm down."

Nate peered into the woods at the edge of Garrett's lawn. Sunlight streamed through the trees bathing the ground in soft light. Birds sang and flitted from tree to tree. It seemed harmless enough, but there was no visible path.

"Fine, but if we get lost in the woods I'm gonna kill you," Nate said.

Lindsey laughed and plunged into the unknown. Garrett and Nate followed her in, hiking in single file. Low-growing brush grabbed at their bare legs and small saplings tried to slap their bodies as they pushed past. The further they walked the thicker the vegetation became and the sunlight was squeezed, giving way to long shadows. The ground was spongy with long-dead leaves and pine needles that covered the secrets of the forest floor.

Nate considered suggesting that they turn back and ask an adult for a ride. He wasn't scared of the woods, or least not too much, but this all seemed inconvenient. Hadn't this sage of the paranormal ever heard of video chat?

Lindsey pulled up short and held her hand up, "Did you guys hear that?"

The boys slid to a stop to avoid crashing into her back. They all stood motionless, straining to hear the sounds of the woods.

"What?" Garrett asked.

"Shh, listen," she said.

There was a slight rustling of undergrowth to their right. Nate could see the thick carpet of forest debris move ever so slightly. A small snake slithered out from under the cover and shot directly at them. Garrett and Nate jumped aside, but Lindsey did not move. She watched the creature dart under a small bush and smiled.

"Cute, right?"

Nate shook his head. "That scared the crap out of me!"

Garrett clutched his chest. "I thought we were goners!"

"Oh, you guys," Lindsey said in a sing-song voice to tease them. "It's just a little baby bull snake."

"OK, well, I don't want to meet his mother," Garrett said.

"Or his father and siblings," Nate added.

"That cave isn't around here, is it?" Garrett asked.

Lindsey sighed. "I've looked all over this area and couldn't find any kind of cave. But who knows, maybe it's hidden under some of these bushes."

"Well, that's a great thought," Garrett said.

A cloud moved across the sun plunging them into a deep shadow of cool air. Nate felt like eyes were on them. He slowly scanned the dense trees. His heart thumped, alerting him to danger. Lindsey and Garrett were searching the surroundings and he knew they felt it too.

"Come on, let's go," Lindsey said in a hushed tone.

They started walking again; the ground crunched like dry bones beneath their feet. They started down a sharp decline and had to grab onto the vegetation to keep from sliding all the way down. A vision of Mel sliding down a rain-slicked embankment jumped into Nate's thoughts. He remembered the sound of the tree branch sticking into her thigh with a wet, sucking sound.

"Be careful, you guys," he said.

Lindsey was first to hit the level ground at the bottom of the hill. The trees were more spaced apart here, but the thick branches overhead kept the sunlight at bay. She turned to face the boys and held her arms wide.

"Almost there, chickens," she said.

The scrub bushes behind her exploded in an uproar of movement. A titanic black cloud of harsh cries and agitated wings rose over their heads. Instinctively, Lindsey ducked and held her hands over her head. Nate stood open-mouthed at the mass of crows.

"Let's go!" Garrett shouted. He ran to Lindsey, grabbed her arm and started running.

Nate felt like his feet were glued to the spot. His brain was shouting at him to run, but his muscles were not getting the message. He had the distinct feeling of someone standing too close to his back, the curious feeling of your personal bubble being popped.

"Nate!" Lindsey shouted.

His body responded to her voice. He sprinted up to them and slowed his pace to match theirs. With Lindsey between them, Nate and Garrett grabbed an arm and pulled her to meet their long-legged stride. Gasping for air, they burst out of the woods onto the shoulder of a narrow two-way road. A crow swiped overhead and landed on a fence post on the other side of the road. His feathers were fluffed out and he shrieked at them. Lindsey shook with laughter.

"What the hell, Linds? What was that?" Garrett panted.

"Just birds, you guys."

"Why did they attack us?" Nate said.

"They didn't. We just scared them. Your bravery is clearly wearing off on me," she said.

"We scared them? Well, whatever. I'm not doing that again," Garrett said. "OK, OK! Chill out, dude!" he shouted at the crow.

"Where are we?" Nate asked looking up and down the lonely stretch of asphalt.

The side they stood on was bordered by the woods. The other side of the road was flat with nothing to block the view of the mountains beyond except for a grazing cow or two. Nate rationalized that the strange sensation he felt in the woods must have been his imagination, but he would have been very happy to move to the other side of the road, away from the woods.

"Right where we need to be," Lindsey said. She pointed up the road with her peacock feather tattooed finger.

A small sign on the wooded side of the road stood with the letters "RTD" at the top.

She smiled at the boys. "Bus stop."

# CHAPTER FOURTEEN

Nate wasn't sure about this; his parents thought he was hanging out at Garrett's. They would have coronaries if they knew where he was going. The trees behind them occasionally rustled and birds (at least Nate hoped they were birds) and messages were screeched from tree to tree. He checked his phone again, two minutes later than last time.

"I thought you said the next bus was in ten minutes?" Nate pointed to the time published on the board next to the stop.

"It's the bus, dude. The scheduled time is just a suggestion," she said.

"So do you give your money to the driver or what?" Garrett asked.

"Oh my God, seriously? Haven't you ever ridden the bus?" Lindsey said.

Garrett and Nate shook their heads.

"Well, then this will be a lesson on urban survival," she laughed.

A phone call would definitely have been a better option. They had already walked at least two miles out of their subdivision to find the bus stop and now they had been waiting for over fifteen minutes. Just as Nate was about to suggest a different course that didn't include marching through the woods, a large white bus with blue and orange striping appeared on the road and lumbered toward them.

With each stop, the empty bus filled up. By the time the suburbs faded to urban buildings and busy streets of Denver every seat was two deep and several people stood in the aisle. Nate smelled everything from body odor to cigarettes to perfume and back again. Much to Nate's relief, at the 16th Street outdoor pedestrian mall in downtown they exited the bus.

The mall was a man-made canyon of towering store fronts. Some of the names Nate recognized, others were obscure and he vaguely wondered how they stayed in business. The nicer restaurants had small patios jutting out onto the pedestrian walkway.

The mall, which had once been a busy downtown street, but was now closed to road traffic, was clogged with people trying to get their weekend started. Nate stared at a girl with fuzzy hot pink leggings doing an impromptu performance with a hula-hoop smack in the middle of the throng. Sweat, food, and car exhaust filled the air; he was beginning to appreciate the fresh air of Dark Pine.

They threaded their way through the crowds to a side street which wasn't much more than an alleyway between two buildings. They came out on a street lined with some old buildings that were occupied by an eclectic group of businesses. Above the electric blue door that they were headed for the words "The Delphic Maxims" glowed in bright blue neon. Based on that name it was impossible for Nate to guess what kind of business it was.

"Hey kid, you got some money?" Nate hadn't seen the man bundled up in a dirty blanket sitting on the sidewalk.

"No, man. Sorry."

"Screw you rich kid! Your daddy cut off your allowance, you little creep? Your damn shoes cost more money than I see in ten years!"

"Chill, dude."

Lindsey grabbed Nate's arm and pulled him along. Her hands were small but surprisingly strong. His stomach did a flip-flop thing.

"Somebody ought to poke your eyes out!" the homeless man shouted after them.

"Making friends, I see," Garrett laughed.

"Shut up." *Why would he say that*? Poke your eyes out. Replace them with soulless black glass. He shook his head and focused on the warmth from Lindsey's hand.

Lindsey let go of Nate's arm and pushed the blue door open. They stepped into a narrow room.

The two large windows in the front of the store were covered with black paint and the main source of light came from the old-school video games that lined the walls. Looking like oversized ATMs, Nate knew some of the titles: Centipedes, Pac Man, and Asteroids. The dark carpet felt crunchy but weirdly spongy under their feet as they moved deeper into the room toward an area of card tables. Each perfect square of a table had four chairs, all pushed in and precisely in the middle of the table legs on either side. A floor to ceiling wooden bookcase covered most of the back wall and its shelves were packed tightly with comic books, action figures, and fantasy card games.

Lindsey told them to wait there and she disappeared through a narrow door. Garrett elbowed Nate and pointed to a small case, like one used in jewelry stores.

Chinese throwing stars glinted in the harsh light of the case. Nate could see the case also contained crystals, odd jewelry, dream catchers, and other trinkets. Several wooden boxes of different sizes sat on top of the case. A small handprinted sign leaning in front of the biggest box announced it as a Vampire Hunting Kit yours for only $1500.00

The boys looked at each other.

"Where the hell are we?" Garrett said.

Nate shook his head. "What do you think is in a vampire hunting kit?"

Garrett smiled. "Let's find out."

They practically jumped to the display and Garrett lifted the top of the biggest box. The hinges creaked like a vampire's coffin in an old movie. A large gold crucifix dominated the velvet-covered interior of the lid, held in place by an elastic band. A wooden mallet, wood stakes, a mirror, a rosary, and three glass vials were stored in the bottom of the box. Each of the vials was labeled in the same precise handwriting as the for sale sign, garlic, blessed salt, and holy water.

"Whoa! Think we need one of these?" Garrett breathed.

Nate was about to answer when the narrow door banged open and Lindsey came back in with an older woman following her. The woman had a shock of flowing white hair that contrasted heavily with her smooth complexion. She looked like she should be working at the cosmetic counter of a high-end department store. She wore a lime green sweater and a zebra print scarf framed her face. Bare feet peeked out from a pair of white jeans. Nate cringed at the thought of bare feet on the carpet.

"Guys, this is Lydia. She owns this place. Lydia, this is Nate and Garrett," Lindsey said.

"Hello gentlemen, it's very nice to meet you," Lydia said.

"Really cool shop," Garrett said.

"Well, thanks. It's my retirement project," she said.

"I used to hang out here when my parents were married. We lived one street over in a high-rise," Lindsey said.

"You practically lived here! She would beat the heck out of anyone on the video games. When she started playing the card games even grown men couldn't beat her," Lydia said to the boys.

Lindsey's cheeks burned red.

"She soaked up every bit of conversation that happened. Believe me, some of the conversations around here can get pretty exceptional, but she kept up with all of it. Soon, she was the expert."

"Well, not expert enough. That's why we're here. It's actually quite exciting, but these guys have seen B-E-Ks. Multiple times!"

Lydia raised her eyebrows. "Interesting."

"Tell her, you guys."

Garrett repeated the story with Nate filling in where needed. Lydia shook her head knowingly and offered the occasional hmm. When they finished the telling, she stared at each of them without speaking for a moment as if she was weighing the validity of their characters.

"Lindsey is right. Brian Bethel the reporter was the first to speak openly. But these things have been seen for thousands of years, I suspect. Brian was approached by two kids who wanted him to give them a ride. Like you guys, he didn't notice at first that their eyes were solid black."

"What happened to him?" Garrett asked.

"Nothing. They scared him shitless and he drove off."

Nate coughed. By the looks of her, he hadn't expected a swear word to come out of this lady, but then he remembered his strange surroundings.

Lydia didn't seem to notice. "I've never heard of a cluster of sightings or repeat sightings like you have experienced."

"OK, so what are they? Why are we seeing them?" Nate asked.

"I don't think anyone really knows what they are. Aliens, hallucinations, inter-dimensional travelers, and vampires are all suggestions that people have come up with. As far as for why, I have no idea."

"I thought about a tupla, maybe. But maybe it is just kids out to prank people because they've heard the stories?" Lindsey offered.

"It could be either," Lydia said.

"No way. The kid I saw covered the 200 feet between us in split second, not even Nate runs that fast. And then there was the sense it gave me. Like being hypnotized or something," Garrett said.

Nate nodded and added his story about them knocking on the second-floor window.

"Did you say tup-something?" Garrett asked Lindsey.

"It's a theory that intense thoughts can produce a physical manifestation. There have been some experiments done where people are told a story of a haunting, totally made up. But then everyone sees the supposed ghost," Lydia answered.

"Isn't that just the power of suggestion?" Nate asked.

"Sort of. But people who were not part of the original experiment, like years later, still see the entity. Maybe so many people have heard of these kids that they have actually materialized from thoughts," Lindsey said.

"I don't know, guys. I'm having a hard time getting my head around this," Nate said.

"I know, it all seems a little crazy, doesn't it? What do you feel they are, Nate?" Lydia asked.

She loosened her scarf as if the room were getting too hot. Nate caught a glimpse of a delicate tattoo of a peacock starting just above her clavicle, the tail feathers hidden in her shirt.

"I don't know. I was hoping you could tell us."

Lydia laughed. "I see. 'Consult the wise' does not mean you will have the answers handed to you."

"They ask for permission to come in. Maybe they're vampires or demons," Garrett said.

"So what? We need some stakes? Holy water?" Nate asked thinking of the cases for sale. This was the weirdest conversation he had ever had. But taking everything, whether he wanted to admit or not, something supernatural was happening.

"Do you know if anyone has ever let them in?" Lindsey asked.

"Not that I know of. But if they did and something terrible happened they wouldn't be around to tell the story, would they?"

A terrible thought occurred to Nate. "The night of the door accident at school, the guy said he heard kids asking to come in. What if the guy who was killed let them in?"

Lindsey stared at him open-mouthed.

"Oh crap. That means they have permission to be in our school," Garrett said.

"Don't get too far ahead of yourselves, kids. In some of the sightings in other cultures these creatures are like a warning sign of trouble. Someone sees one and a flood hits, that sort of thing."

"Well, so far Missy has gotten hurt, and a poor door installer is dead. I'd say that's trouble," Nate said.

"But what if they aren't just messengers and they are causing the problems?" Garrett asked, giving voice to the thing hanging between them.

"Then we gotta figure out how to make them go away or protect ourselves somehow," Nate said.

They all turned to Lydia.

"Have you talked to your parents?" she asked.

Garrett shook his head.

"My parents would put me in therapy so fast I wouldn't know what hit me," Nate said.

Lydia nodded knowingly. "I'm no expert, no one is, but I could ask around. I have a couple of regulars that might be helpful. In the meantime, take these." She held out tiny silver medals in the palm of her hand.

"What are those?" Lindsey asked.

"Saint Christopher medals." Lydia shrugged.

Lindsey said, "I didn't think you believed that religious iconography meant anything."

A shadow passed over Lydia's face. "It couldn't hurt. Take them, keep in them in your pocket. I'll ask around for help. Maybe they'll just quit showing up."

Garret sighed. "What do we do until then?"

"Hold it together. And, oh, don't let them in," Lydia said.

"No kidding," Nate and Garrett said in unison.

It was getting late. The thought of hanging out at a bus stop in the dark did not appeal to Nate in the least. A walk back through the woods in the dark was not going to happen. He couldn't call his parents for a ride, but Lindsey arranged for her dad to get them on his way home from work. He worked nearby at a bank and had a late meeting. They didn't have to wait long before an expensive, shiny, black SUV pulled to the curb and honked. Lindsey climbed in shotgun and Nate and Garrett got in the back.

"Thanks for the ride, Mr. Pyre," Garrett said.

"Sure, Garrett. I'm Lindsey's dad, Matt Pyre," he said eyeing Nate from the rear view mirror.

"Dad, this is Nate, from school," Lindsey said.

"Nice to meet you, Nate."

"You too, sir."

The SUV glided from the curb and they rode home mostly in silence. Each one lost in their thoughts.

After dropping off Nate and Garrett, Lindsey and Matt drove further into Dark Pine to their house. It was in the Backcountry, not far from Garrett.

"What were you guys doing at Lydia's?" Mike asked.

"Just messing around."

"Hm, Nate seems like a nice kid."

"He is. His family just moved here and his dad works for Garrett's dad."

"Oh."

"What?"

"Nothing," Matt smiled.

When Lindsey opened the door from the garage to the mudroom, warm smells of food welcomed her home. Mona, her stepmom, wiped her hands on her apron as she leaned over to peek inside the oven. Kimberli sat at the oversized island tearing lettuce and tossing it in a bowl.

"Normal people have like a cook and a housekeeper. Why do we have to do all the work?" Kimberli said.

"You guys are a bit late," Mona said, ignoring Kimberli.

"We ran Garrett home and um, what was his name?"

"Dad! You know his name is Nate," Lindsey said.

Matt laughed, "I'm kidding. We ran Garrett and Nate home."

"Nate? Nate Camden?" Kimberli said.

"Yep, I guess," Matt said as he leaned in to kiss Mona on the cheek.

"Gross," Kimberli mumbled.

They ate dinner to Matt's recounting of the big meeting from that afternoon. Somewhere between asset-backed securities and over-collateralization Lindsey's thoughts turned to what Nate and Garrett had seen. She glanced out the floor-to-ceiling window in the dining room to the woods beyond.

The outdoor landscape lighting in the backyard did little to penetrate the darkness. She could make out dark shapes of trees but in the darkness she couldn't see past the first row that stood on the property line. Anything could lurk out there and no one would ever know. She wondered who, or what, may have watched her this summer as she traipsed around looking for the legendary cave. Maybe it wasn't so legendary

"Earth to Lindsey," Kimberli's voice brought her back to the table.

"What?"

"Dishes, your turn," Matt said.

Matt helped Lindsey gather the plates and set them in the sink. She began to rinse them off and arrange them in the dishwasher. It was just her luck they ate lasagne on her dish night.

Kimberli settled on the same stool she had been sitting on to make the salad. "What were you doing with Garrett and Nate?"

"Nothing, just hanging out."

"My mom was getting worried. You guys should have like called."

Lindsey kept her back to Kimberli and kept placing dishes in the racks, making sure they clanged loudly.

"You know my mom has been burned before. I don't want to see her hurt again," Kimberli said.

"My dad's not going to cheat on her if that's what you're worried about."

It was, a little. Her mother had learned nothing from the first failed marriage, as far as Kimberli was concerned. Mona never wore makeup, her idea of a hairstyle was a ponytail, and she only ever seemed to wear workout clothes. It was Mona's fault they had been abandoned the first time. Kimberli would not let that happen again if she could help it.

"Of course not. So, like where were you guys that Dad had to give you a ride?" Kimberli said.

"My dad gave us a ride from downtown."

"Eww, downtown is so ghetto. I'm sure Nate was impressed."

"Well, it beats sitting at home."

"I had practice tonight for your information. Some of us have lives you know."

"No, I didn't know." Lindsey continued to bang dishes into the dishwasher.

"You know, Lindsey, you try to be like all edgy and stuff with your blue hair and tattoo, but seriously you, should embrace your inner dork. It would be less embarrassing."

Lindsey turned to face her and shrugged. "I am what I am."

"And what you are is fat."

Lindsey raised her eyebrows. "Oooooh, real original. I can't help it if you're jelly of my curves."

"Whatever, Linds. Keep like telling yourself that." Kimberli slid off the stool. "Nate could never be interested in anyone like you. Stop like trying so hard. It makes you look desperate. I swear, I'm embarrassed to be related to you."

Lindsey narrowed her eyes. "Like, right back atcha."

Kimberli clicked her tongue and whisked out of the kitchen. Lindsey turned back to the sink, letting the warm water pour over her hands and took deep breaths. One of these days she was going to flip out and strangle that little Barbie wannabe.

A sharp click of something hitting the window in the dining room drew her attention. Thoughts of kids with black eyes jumped into her mind. A sensation in her chest made her breath come in short gasps. Tiptoeing, she slunk to the dining room and peeked around the doorway. The space beyond the window was a black void. She jumped when a second ping came from the window. She hadn't been hearing things.

Lindsey eased toward the window like a bird wary of a feeder. The yard beyond the window was still. Nothing moving, only lawn furniture and flower beds filled with blooms that looked vulnerable against the night. Lindsey stood motionless, scanning the area for anything. A small bush in front of the window rustled. Her body tensed.

A large dark shape lumbered out of the bush and across the yard toward the woods. A thick ringed tail was the last thing to disappear into the thicket.

Lindsey let her breath out. "Dang you, Mr. Raccoon." Her head felt light with relief and she went back to start the dishwasher.

## CHAPTER FIFTEEN

No one would blame Linda for taking the day off. Besides, it wasn't like she was taking it to goof around. Ben needed to make arrangements at his office so he could take the next few days to be with Inna, and Linda offered to stay at the hospital. The doctors still had no idea what was wrong with her. The specialist was leaning toward something viral at this point.

Linda stopped by school to set up a few things for her sub, then went to the teacher's lounge to scrub her hands one more time before she left. She had washed her hands so many times in past few days that her skin was dry and irritated. Better to have itchy hands than what Inna had.

"Miss Garza?"

She jumped. "Oh, Mr. Greene, you startled me. I didn't expect anyone to be here so early."

"Sorry. I'm usually here early. There's a lot to do getting a new school off the ground."

"Yes, I'm sure."

"I saw your request for a sub. Hope you're not sick." He knew she wasn't.

"No. I'm taking a personal day. Mrs. Kerpin's husband has asked me to keep her company today because he can't be there."

"Yes, I spoke to him yesterday evening. I understand she is quite ill. Had to put in for a long-term sub. Terrible this early in the year. Terrible to have so many subs in the building on the same day so early in the year. The more subs students have, the lower their test scores," he said.

"I'll be back tomorrow," Linda said.

"Oh, I know. It's just a tough thing so early in the year. Having too many subs in the building is so disruptive, especially for new teachers with the new pay-for-performance in place and all." He mopped his forehead with a handkerchief.

"Technically, I'm not new," she said.

"Well, I meant new to the district."

"It really can't be helped. I'm allowed three personal days, Mr. Greene."

"Oh, of course, I'm just musing out loud. There is something you could do for me, however."

"And that is?"

"Mrs. Kerpin was heading the Fall Carnival, now that she won't be able to see that through I was hoping you could take it over for her."

"What would that entail?" Linda figured it really wouldn't matter just as he wasn't really asking.

"Most of the planning is done. There's a terrific group of parent volunteers heading it up. It would be your job to coordinate things, help them with whatever they need, that sort of thing."

"Sure. I'd be happy to help out."

"Wonderful. I'll email you the info. See you tomorrow."

She fought the urge to stick her tongue out at his back.

Visitors to Inna's room were required to suit up in a paper gown, shoe covers, plastic gloves, and face mask. Linda suited up and was just inside the door when her phone vibrated in her back pocket. She dashed back to the hallway and slipped her facemask down under her chin.

"Hello?"

"Lin, please don't hang up," a male voice said.

She felt her chest tighten. "I told you not to call."

"I know. I'm sorry. Please, can't we just talk?"

"Now you want to talk? It's way too late for any of that, Josh."

"Linda, come on. I'm trying to say I'm sorry for all that. I'll go back to counseling. I don't want things to end this way. I don't want things to end. I love you."

She winced. "Look, I'm just trying to move forward. I think we established that I couldn't do that with you. It's too hard. You are too hard."

"OK, I admit it. I handled everything in the worst possible way. Can't you forgive me?"

"It's not about forgiveness. It's about trust and respect. I just can't. Please, leave me alone." She stabbed the phone with slightly shaking hands.

"Everything OK?" Ben asked. He was coming down the hallway with a paper coffee cup in his hand.

"Um, yes, just a-" she took a deep breath. "Nothing. How's she doing today?"

"They put her on anti-viral medications. We ended up having to sedate her last night."

"What? Why?"

He let out a heavy breath and loosened the scarf around his neck. "After you left I was getting ready to run by our house and take a shower. She totally freaked out. Hysterical about some kids that we all had to watch out for. She was shouting and trying to get out of bed. Then she, well, it's kind of embarrassing."

"Ben? What?"

He ran his hand through his hair. "She was spewing off about vampires or something."

"I'm sure it's mostly just the fever and dehydration, don't you think?"

"I'm sure. But it was freaky. She was dead serious. I've never seen her like that before."

"She told me about vampires and kids being at the house, pranking her," Linda said.

"I don't know what to think. Well, look I really have to get home, shower, and get to my office. Thanks for staying with her. Call me if anything changes."

"I will."

Linda went into Inna's room and slouched down in the vinyl recliner. Oxygen hissed from a tube into a mask on Inna's face and the rhythmic beeping of the heart monitor were the only sounds in the room. Linda wrinkled her nose and wondered just how well the facemask worked. Hospitals had a distinctive smell she could hardly stomach, the smell of pain.

Like something out of Dr. Frankenstein's laboratory, the head of the bed began a mechanical climb. Inna was awake now, but her eyes were in deep shadow and bloodshot. She slipped the oxygen mask down.

"Hi," she croaked.

"Hi. Can I get you anything?"

Inna shook her head, "I'm all right. I heard Ben tell you about our night last night."

"Are you OK?"

"Linda, I know how it all sounds, but I'm not losing my mind."

"Inna, you're very ill."

"I know but, Linda it's not the fever talking. I think God is testing me. I left my faith completely when I met Ben. He's against all that kind of thing. Atheist. Just turned my back on it for him. Now he thinks I'm crazy. God is seeing who I'll pick this time. He's allowed the Eritich, or whatever, to cause my illness, to test me." She struggled to get enough breath in to push the words out.

"Inna, I don't why you are sick but some kind of ghost kids nor God is to blame. I'm with Ben on this one."

"You don't believe in God?"

"No. There's too much evil in the world for God to exist. How could He just sit back and let it all happen? No, I don't believe anymore."

"Anymore? But you did once."

"Inna, do we need to talk about this now? You need to rest and put your oxygen back on."

"I will if you tell me why you don't believe anymore."

Linda smiled to hear some of the old Inna come through. "Let's just say that the past couple of years have been kind of tough."

"All right, go on. I'm a captive audience."

Linda let out a defeated sigh. "Listen, you want to hear my sad story of woe, then get well!"

Inna tried to laugh, but it became a strangled hacking cough. She pulled her oxygen mask back on. Linda pulled her chair up next to the bed and straightened Inna's covers.

A small group of nurses bustled into the room. One of them explained that the doctor ordered a CAT scan for Inna and they would take her down in the next few minutes.

A nurse with a wheelchair banged into the room. Linda helped her transfer Inna from the bed to the chair. Linda could feel Inna's ribs poking through her hospital gown and her skin felt shockingly thin. Linda gave Inna's shoulder a soft squeeze before the nurse spun the chair out of the room.

"I'll be here when you get back," Linda called after her.

Inna felt hopelessness creeping up on her like mold that has taken root on a forgotten piece of cheese. After what she had seen she couldn't accept Linda and Ben's viewpoint. There was an abundance of evil in the world but didn't that mean there had to be good too? There was more to the world than what science and intellect could address. She knew that now.

The nurse wheeled her into a large waiting room with two doors on opposite sides. One announced "Imaging" and other "Orthopedic Surgery." Her mind wandered from her predicament and she was thinking how convenient the setup was. X-ray shows a broken arm and then you go right next door to get it fixed.

Too bad she didn't have a broken arm. That would be easy to fix.

When she got back to her room she would ask the chaplain to come to her room; maybe that would be a good place to start. She wasn't sure if she would pass this test or not.

"You wait right here, Mrs. Kerpin. My door key seems to be broken or something," the nurse said.

Inna hadn't even noticed her swiping the key card. She nodded and the nurse left her.

"Miss Kerpin?" She turned to see a face she recognized from school, second period, smart, and always on task, to be exact. Her mind was as sharp as always.

"Nate! What are you doing here?" She was suddenly a little confused.

"My sister. She's having her shoulder fixed today." He nodded toward the "Orthopedic Surgery" door.

"Oh! Oh, I'm so sorry. Is she OK?"

"Yeah, just a torn ligament or something. Are you all right?"

She realized how she must look. "Oh yeah. I'm just having some tests done."

"Oh."

"Don't you worry, I'll be back at school soon. Torturing you with homework and other nasty things."

Nate could hear her breathing was labored. Her eyes were set deep in shadow and her color didn't look quite right.

"I'm sorry you're sick. Hospitals kinda suck."

A faint smile touched her lips. "That they do."

An awkward silence took over, and Nate looked for a polite way to go back to his seat by his mom and his cell phone game.

Before he could find one, her arm shot out like a snake striking out at prey, and she clutched Nate's sleeve. Her lips trembled and her eyes were wide with fear as she stared past him. He slowly turned to see what had frightened her. He saw them. Only for a moment but he saw them. Exactly as they had been at the football game except now, they were both pointing at him.

His guts turned to stone. Ms. Kerpin had seen them too. He looked back at her and her eyes rolled up into her head exposing only the whites. The wheelchair rocked violently with the seizure that was beginning to take hold of her body.

"Help! Mom, Dad, help!"

His parents dropped the magazines they had been reading and rushed to Nate and Inna. A woman in scrubs pushed past them and slammed a red buzzer near the door to the Imaging suites. David helped her lay Inna down on the ground. Mel and Nate tried not to get in the way as a team of medical staff swarmed over Inna.

Nate clutched his mom like his life depended on not losing his grip on her. His ears were buzzing and his mouth had gone dry. They watched the medical personnel load Inna on a gurney and whisk her away.

"I'm sorry you had to see that. Seizures look scarier than they are. Do you know her?" the nurse who pushed the buzzer asked.

"She's our son's teacher," David said.

"You're here for your teacher?"

"No. We just happened to run into her. Our daughter is having shoulder surgery today," David said.

Missy. If those kids, or ghosts, or whatever, were showing themselves to adults there was nothing to keep them safe. Missy was in there, unconscious. What if they showed themselves to the surgeon and everything went to crap? He felt his panic rising.

"Mom."

"It's OK, honey. She must be really sick," she patted his hand.

They all jumped when the orthopedic doors flew open.

"Mr. and Mrs. Camden?" A very tall and thin man in green scrubs with a cap over his hair blew in with the doors.

"Is everything OK?" he asked.

"Yes, there was an emergency out here with another patient. Is Missy, all right?" Mel asked.

"She did great. The tear was minimal and it went much faster than we anticipated. She's in recovery right now and one of you can see her shortly. Then they'll take her to her room."

"That's great news," David said. "You go in Mel. I'll see her up in her room."

"See honey. I told you everything would be fine," Mel said to Nate.

*No, Nate* thought. *Nothing is fine.*

# CHAPTER SIXTEEN

Nate glued himself to his dad while Mel went to see Missy in recovery. Then he glued himself to his mom when they walked back to Missy's room to wait for her.

"She's fine, honey," Mel said when she noticed his odd behavior. "They just want to keep her here a couple hours and then she's coming home. Relax."

Nate nodded. Home would be good, but he knew no place was safe. His skin felt like small insects were crawling all over and a headache was pounding in his temples. He had to talk to somebody. Anybody. Lindsey came to mind.

He stepped out in the hallway and texted her, then he texted Garrett with a message to call him. Nate's phone vibrated almost immediately. He told Garrett everything that happened with Ms. Kerpin.

"That's pretty serious shit. Maybe they're done with us now?"

"I don't know. I hope you're right." He saw a bed being wheeled into Missy's room. "I gotta go, but I'll call you later."

Garrett put his phone down. Thoughts were racing through his mind. He returned to the work on his desk, popsicle stick crosses. The glue would be gone soon, but the thought of leaving the relative safety of his house to buy more was not appealing. Bad enough he would have to go to school on Monday. What if the BEKs were in the school, waiting for them? At least at his house he knew they didn't have permission to be there.

The pleasant chimes of the door bell sounded. Garrett jumped and knocked his projects on the floor, wet glue spilling onto the rug.

"Shit," he muttered.

The bell rang again. He knew he'd have to see who it was. Besides him, only his mom was home and she was in the shower.

He peeked his head out of the bedroom door and listened. His room emptied out onto a catwalk overlooking the two story family room. Not hearing his mom moving to the door, Garrett slunk to the railing and peered into the tasteful and quiet room below. He couldn't see the front door from here, but at the top of the spiral staircase there was a security monitor. The bell rang again, twice, before he got to it.

He groaned. The camera was down and the screen was blank. The bell rang again.

A door slammed. "Garrett! Can't you hear the door?" His mom shuffled across the family room in a robe and her hair wrapped turban style in a towel.

"No! Mom, wait!" He took the stairs two at time, jumped the last four and slid on his stocking feet. He couldn't stop and crashed into her.

"Garrett, what is wrong with you!"

"Mom! Mom, don't open the door!" His eyes wild.

"Don't open the door? What are you talking about?" she said and pushed past him.

"No! Mom!" He grabbed the dangling belt of her robe and jerked her back.

"Garrett! What is wrong with you?"

"Mom, please. Don't open the door."

"It's the pool guy!" She pointed to the security monitor at the bottom of the stairs.

"Oh," he said in a small voice.

"What is the matter with you? Who did you think it was?" she went to the door and pulled it open.

Garrett froze to his spot. His mom finished giving the pool guy instructions and closed the door.

"I don't know what has been up with you lately. Would you care to share?"

"I, um, the monitor was down upstairs."

"OK," she said slowly. "Is there something you need to tell me?"

He shook his head. "Nah, everything is cool, Mom."

"Uh-huh. Well, if you change your mind let me know. I've gotta get some sleep. I'm on at the hospital tonight." She shuffled back to her room and firmly shut the door.

He went back to his task at hand. The glue that was left would have to be enough, no way was he leaving the house unless he had to. After the glue bottle had been scraped clean, he gathered the dry crosses and laid one in each windowsill upstairs. He tested the other makeshift crosses and most were still wet, but he couldn't wait much longer, it would be dark soon. He gently carried his handiwork to the basement. Several crosses had to be straightened before he could leave them in a window sill. He had no idea what to do about the doors; garlic, maybe. His mom would notice that. Garrett realized that there weren't enough crosses for the windows on the main floor. Maybe none of this was necessary. They had to be invited in, didn't they? Maybe they weren't vampires or demons and crosses, holy water, and garlic were a waste of time. Maybe nothing would stop them until...what?

He couldn't explain how he knew the beings wanted more, and would not leave until they got what they came for. Garrett wasn't sure exactly what they wanted, but it was more than injury and sickness. He thought that might leave one thing- death.

A shiver moved through him and he sprinted up the stairs to his room. He closed the door, took a marker off his desk and drew a cross on the inside. Better safe than sorry.

# CHAPTER SEVENTEEN

All Sophia could hope for was to get by unnoticed, but she wasn't enthusiastic. She didn't know if the confessions page was still being flooded with terrible things. She had turned off her phone and computer after cleaning up the garage door and had not turned them back on. With some acting, she had convinced her dad she was sick and was able to miss school for a couple of days, but if she pushed it another day, he'd make her go to the doctor. Not even with an academy award worthy performance would she be able to hide her secret from a doctor's exam.

Sophia decided that she would concentrate on getting from class to class. She couldn't think ahead to cheer practice. It had crossed her mind she should just quit, and facing the prospect of actually going made it more than a passing idea. She stood as far away from the other kids as possible. Trying to disappear, she pressed herself against the tree that she had spoken to her mom under a few days ago. That seemed like months ago. She absently picked away at the light pink polish on her nails.

Desperately, she scanned the building looking for a door she might use to slip in. One of the side doors that was used for before-school care for the younger students stood open. A small girl with the same curly hair as Garrett was holding the door. Sophia moved so she could see who the door was being opened for. Maybe this was her answer. If she hurried she could slip in right behind the person. The door swung shut before she could get a look or take advantage of the open door.

Refocusing her gaze, she caught sight of a girl with long dark corkscrew hair swinging from side to side as she walked. Her arm was in a sling and she headed directly for Sophia. Her heart leaped and some of the pressure building in her head released.

"Missy!" Sophia took a step toward her, but the look on Missy's face stopped her cold.

"Don't even, Sophia. I thought we were friends! Kimberli told me what you have been saying about me since I've been out!"

Sophia shrunk back. "What are you talking about?"

"How the squad was stronger without me. That if I can't even hold my balance in a simple extension then I shouldn't be on the JV team. That the best thing about me being hurt was you got to be around my stupid brother!" Tears welled up in Missy's eyes, "That my hair is ugly and I should have it straightened so I would fit in better! Really, Sophia?"

"Missy, I never...I wouldn't!"

"The other girls all say they heard you! Are you saying they are all liars?"

"Missy, no. I mean, yes!"

"Right. My brother doesn't even like you. When he hears what you said he'll hate you."

"No, Missy! We are friends. I would never say that stuff."

"You know what I think? I think you're the liar. Just like your crack-head mother!" Missy spun on her heel and marched to the waiting group of girls that had gathered a few yards away.

Sophia felt like she had been kicked in the chest by a mule. She had shared the thing about her mom with Missy because they were friends. Missy was her only real friend. Now she didn't even have that. She had been gutted in front of the whole school with all of her secrets spilling out for them to examine.

The bell rang.

She hugged her backpack and dropped her head, trying to disguise herself behind her hair. Kids were rushing past her, but no one seemed especially interested in her. Maybe other kids in the school didn't even care, maybe she was as invisible to them as they were to her.

She slunk to her locker and opened it. Hanging from the shelf was a package of old style rectangular razor blades, the kind you screwed into a handle. A note taped to the bottom of the package: *Thought you could use these*!

She hadn't realized that a group of kids had gathered behind her to witness the show. Their laughter startled her. She slammed the locker shut and ran for any escape that would present itself.

As if signaling the end of the first round, the bell rang again and the halls emptied. Sophia headed for the one place she knew no one would be right now, the locker room. When she got there, it was indeed empty. No one had gym first period except for the elementary kids. They didn't use the locker room, but someone might come in to use the bathroom.

She threw herself into a shower stall and yanked the curtain shut. Her body shook as if she were in the arctic without a coat. She slid to the floor before her unsteady legs dropped her. Splotches of water covered the floor, and she felt it soak her pants. Deep heaves rose from her chest and she couldn't help but take big gulps of the damp air.

She heard the locker room door click open and she put her hand over her mouth to stifle her breathing. Whispers. A giggle. Footfalls came directly to the shower stall. Sophia held her breath.

"I can help you if you let me."

It was a boy, but it didn't sound like Nate or Garrett.

"Please, Miss. Let me help you."

*Miss*? It couldn't be. She sucked in a sharp breath.

"I can help you if you let me," he said again.

The voice was so soothing. Why was she frightened by this before? She felt herself relax, but tears escaped her eyes.

"Everything will be fine if you let me in."

Fine. Yes, she wanted that more than anything. Her trembling hand reached for the shower curtain.

"All you have to do is let me in. Please, can't I come in?"

Sophia clutched the corner of the shower curtain in a fist so tight her knuckles went white. She dragged it slowly, almost imperceptibly aside. A pair of old-fashioned brown dress shoes and the bottom of pant legs were revealed. *See? No, claws.*

Her heart was pounding in her ears. Somewhere a small voice was trying to shout at her to stop but she couldn't.

"This won't take long," he said.

She hesitated. *What won't take long?*

The door to the locker room banged open. She jumped and dropped the curtain. A rush of noisy girls entered the room with laughter and banging of locker doors. She peeked out of the stall. No one was standing where the boy, or whatever, had been seconds before. It wasn't possible that she had been in here for the whole fifty-five-minute period, was it? An overwhelming urge to run washed over her.

She sprang from the stall and dashed out of the locker room. Girls squealed in surprise, but she never looked back. Her body was shaking again and her stomach was in revolt. The hallway was a river of kids moving to their next class. She pressed herself up against the wall as faces flooded past her.

Looking for another escape, she caught sight of a small sign sticking out from above a doorway. She pushed her way through to that tiny spot of hope.

"Hi, Sweetie. You OK?" the plump blonde-haired lady at the nurse's desk asked.

"No. I think I ate something bad."

Frowning, the woman jumped up and in a jangle of bracelets put her hand to Sophia's forehead.

"You're freezing! Grab that blanket there and lie down while I call your mom."

"My dad," Sophia mumbled as she let the woman guide her to cot inside a small room behind her desk.

"Lewis, right?" she returned to the outer office.

Sophia felt relieved to be in the brightly lit place with people who knew her name. She heard the woman dialing a phone and then she heard a familiar voice that made her heart jump.

"I just need a Band-Aid, no biggie. Caught it with a stapler," Garrett said.

"A stapler? How exactly did you accomplish that? Never mind, I don't want to know," the nurse laughed. "Give me a sec, OK? I need to make this call, but my phone isn't working. Go in there and run it under some cold water. Band-Aids are on the counter."

"A stapler? What are you? Two-years-old?" It was a girl's voice Sophia didn't recognize.

With a rustling, Garrett came into the small infirmary to use the sink. When he saw Sophia, his face lit up with a broad smile.

The BEKs, as he had come to call them, hadn't shown up to anyone since Nate and Ms. Kerpin saw them in the hospital. His mom told him that Ms. Kerpin was in a coma, and maybe it was mean, but he hoped the BEKs were satisfied with that. Seeing Sophia alive and well reaffirmed his belief that the weird episode was over.

"Hey! Where have you been? I've texted you like a hundred times..." His voice trailed off when he took in her pallid face.

"Sick, I've been sick."

The sight of his friendly curly hair and the way he seemed to be happy to see her was too much. She felt like sobbing. There was real concern in his eyes. She had an urge to get up and hug him. Feeling his arms around her would bring her back from the cliff she was perched on. The warmth of his body would ripple life back into her. She could learn to skateboard; with all her gymnastic training she could probably do some crazy tricks.

A pretty girl with short black hair, bright blue glasses, and a black sweater that was bulging with well-placed curves popped in.

"Come on stapler-boy. Get that thing under some water," she said. She grabbed his hand and led him to the sink.

Lindsey held Garrett's hand under the running water and Sophia noticed how they pressed themselves against each other, talking in hushed tones.

Her insides hollowed out.

"All better," Garrett grinned and held up his bandaged finger. "We gotta go. Call me later if you feel better, OK? Some stuff has happened and I need to talk to you."

She nodded. Rolling over on her side she curled up into a tight ball. Why didn't she yank that damn curtain open? She didn't know what would have happened, but it had to be better than this.

# CHAPTER EIGHTEEN

Inna had been on Linda's mind all day. Ben phoned her before school to give her an update. Her vitals were stable, but she was still in a coma. The doctors did not understand why she had a seizure or how it ended with her in a coma. None of the tests gave any answers. It was inconceivable that someone so young and perfectly healthy less than a few days ago could have ended up in this state. It was a hard thing to witness.

Linda had come here for a fresh start, to escape the pain of the past. But heartache seemed to follow her like a stray dog. Maybe she caused it all. She had the reoccurring feeling that her life was somehow cursed, restitution from wrongs in a previous life.

Linda thought back to the last conversation she had with Inna. Inna said God was testing her because she had left her faith. Linda had done the same, not just left her faith but her life. If all of this was a test for her, she had failed pretty soundly.

She sighed heavily. It had been a long few days. The fall festival turned out to be a bigger project than she hoped. The few student helpers she recruited were turning out not to be a lot of help. She'd sent Garrett around earlier to hang banners and he stapled his finger before he even got one done. Thankfully more parents had been emailing her, willing to step up in light of Ms. Kerpin's illness.

The festival was open to the entire community. It was a way to show off the new building and raise funds for the things that the school wanted but the budget wouldn't cover. Most of the staff had been very helpful when asked to sponsor a student-led carnival booth. The only resistance came when she needed volunteer targets for the pie-throwing booth. The only other hiccup had been when the cheerleaders wanted to have a kissing booth. Linda was able to convince their coach and sponsor that it was unsanitary. She wasn't sure if the hugging booth alternative they came up with was totally appropriate but Mr. Greene had given his approval.

The bell rang bringing her attention back to her last period class. Seats were full and heads were bent doing the warm-up assignment she had posted on the Smartboard. Her eyes went to the one unoccupied seat that was assigned to Sophia. Empty again. She felt a small constriction at the base of her heart.

She had come so close to telling Inna about the empty seat that had changed her life forever. Like a jack-in-the-box wound too far, the memories sprang into her mind. The girl with a ten-thousand-watt smile and chocolate skin swirled into focus.

From the first day this girl showed up in her class, Linda knew she had potential. The more she got to know Yvette, the more deeply she got involved.

Yvette's home life was a mess and Linda felt that with the right support Yvette could overcome it. Linda sank money, time, and effort into this girl. In retrospect, she knew she overstepped a professional boundary, but she didn't care. Her ex-husband knew it too and moved from annoyed to angry.

Linda had agreed to go away to Mexico with her husband for the holiday and she didn't have any contact with Yvette over winter break. When they returned, Yvette seemed very withdrawn. Then one day, her seat was empty and it remained that way for several days. The attendance secretary and Linda tried to call home, but they were unable to get in contact with anyone. They alerted the school resource officer who made contact with the mother. She thought Yvette had run away. Anger boiled in her at this memory. How does your kid go missing and you just shrug it off? Relieved for one less mouth to feed, disgusting.

"Miss, something smells bad," a boy who sat next to the storage room door told her.

She walked over and the scent coming from under the door made her gag. She thought a mouse or something must have died in there. It would have to be a very large mouse to smell this bad. She rummaged around in her desk for the key to the door but couldn't find it. She called the custodian for help.

"Wow, that stinks!" he proclaimed when he got close enough to put his key in the lock.

From here, the memory always goes into slow-motion. The lock tumblers click, the door is pulled open, no light spills into the small room. Linda puts her hand to face to block the stench. The custodian flips on the light. Dangling feet clad in worn out Chuck Taylors. Linda's eyes follow the feet up a body to a swollen purple face that once lit up the room.

Linda felt her chest constrict.

"Ms. Garza?"

She blinked the tears back and refocused on a boy standing in front of her.

"We're done with the warm-up," he said.

She pushed the memories down and cleared her throat. "All right, great." She swiped the tears under each eye. "Allergies." She cleared her throat again. "Today we're going to talk about a very specific type of story-telling, urban legends," she said.

There was a small collective sigh of approval.

For the introduction, she told her students the stories of several popular urban legends. Once she entered teacher-mode, her focus became laser sharp on her students and the lesson. A respite from her sick friend and dark thoughts.

The photos for each story she projected on the Smartboard were a big hit. Linda took a moment to glance around at the captive audience as they studied the photo of an oversized alligator supposedly found in the sewers of New York City.

She walked around each table as she told the stories, gauging students' reactions and engagement in the lesson. Garrett was doodling on his notebook as she talked. Linda leaned in to get a look at his drawing. One of the sketches was a pretty good cartoon of an alligator peering out from a toilet. She was about to ask him to share it, but when she saw his current doodle she stopped talking.

It was a boy in a long sleeved shirt with spiked hair and black shark eyes. What Inna said to her about the eyes of the kids that harassed her jumped to the front of her mind.

She put her hand on Garrett's shoulder. "I need to see you for a quick minute after class, OK?"

Garrett looked startled, "OK."

Nate gave Garrett a curious look. Garrett shrugged. It wasn't the first or last time he'd get in trouble for his mind wandering. Linda noted the exchange.

"You too, Nate."

Nate gave Garrett a thanks-a-lot look, and the class hummed with the sounds of pleasure and relief it wasn't them being asked to stay after class.

Nate and Garrett waited in their seats for the other kids to file out after the bell rang. Linda sat on the edge of the table next to theirs and crossed her arms over her chest. She didn't believe that these two were running around scaring a teacher, but maybe they knew who was. The sound of Nate cracking the knuckles on his right hand broke the silence.

"I noticed your drawing, Garrett."

"Oh, well, you know. I was just kinda messing around while you talked. But I swear I was listening to every word."

"Specifically, I found the picture of the boy with black eyes interesting."

Nate dropped his gaze to the table top and Garrett slouched down on himself.

"Have kids been dressing up like that and pranking people?" she asked. Might as well get right to the point.

Nate's head shot up, "Did you see them?"

Linda raised her eyebrows, "No, but other people might have. What do you guys know about it?"

Nate scanned the room as if a clue as to what to say might be found. They could deny knowing anything. That would be easiest. But it could be an opportunity to recruit some adult help. What could he say that wouldn't get him sent to the school psychologist?

He took note that her desk was way over in the corner of the room and that she hardly ever sat there during class time. All the stuff on the walls was created by students instead of the usual classroom posters. She'd always made him feel like his ideas were valid, that what he thought mattered. There was an instance that she called him interesting. No one had ever said that to him before.

"Some of us may have seen these kids messing around. You know, trying to scare people," Nate said.

"Do you guys know what kids?"

Both boys shook their heads.

"We don't know who or what they are or where they come from. Just that for the past few weeks they have been coming up to some of us and asking for stuff," Garrett said.

"Stuff? What stuff?"

"Like to use our phones and stuff," Garrett said.

"That's all we know, Ms. Garza," Nate said.

"Did you say what?" Inna said they weren't human.

"What?" Garrett said.

"No, you said, you didn't know who or what they are."

"Did I? Um, my tongue twisted I guess."

She eyed them both. "Fine. Well, these boys might get someone, or themselves hurt doing what they are doing." She paused to see if they offered up anything else. "I feel like you guys are holding back on me."

"No, Ms. Garza, we really don't know anything more," Garrett said.

"OK. If you hear anything or find out who they are will you let me know right away?"

"Yes ma'am," Nate said.

Linda took a deep breath knowing that was all she would get out them. At least now she could tell Ben that Inna hadn't imagined that part of her ordeal. She opened her mouth to excuse the boys, but the classroom door banged open, and Principal Greene blew in followed by Rick Lewis.

"Sorry to interrupt," Mr. Greene said, but Linda could tell by his briskness he wasn't. "Did Sophia Lewis show up in class today?"

"Sophia? No. She hasn't been in class for the last few days. Is everything all right?"

"Boys, you can go," Mr. Greene dismissed them as he hitched up his trousers.

They both looked at Ms. Garza.

"It's OK boys. You're free to leave," she said.

They stepped out of the room but lingered at the open door to listen to what was going on.

"She's been sick, but she came to school today. Apparently, she was still sick and went to the nurse's office. They called me to come and get her. When I got here she was gone," Rick said.

"Gone?" Linda asked.

"She's even a no-show at cheerleading. I've looked every place I can think she'd be. It's like she vanished," he said.

Nate and Garrett shot each other startled looks. They heard movement toward the door and they both took off.

"I'll call you later," Garrett said.

Nate nodded and hunched his shoulders. For maybe the first time ever in his life, he wished he was heading home and not to practice.

***

"Nate, I'm not sure what is the matter with you but seriously, kid, you need to get it together. You were unfocused and undisciplined here today, a good combination for bench warming. Do you hear me?" The coach practically spit the words into his face.

Nate looked at his shoes. It was true, he had been a disaster out on the field. He couldn't run his routes correctly and even when he managed to do that he couldn't hang onto the ball. Eating turf or looking at the sky from flat on his back was how he spent the majority of the practice.

"Yes, sir," he said.

"OK." The calm before the storm. "Jesus, kid! You're my best player. We can't win with you playing like that! What the hell is wrong with you? Are you sick?"

"No, sir. I, I have no excuse, coach," he mumbled.

Coach forced an angry breath out and slapped his thigh with his ball cap. He jammed it back on his head and fidgeted with it a moment. "I better see some marked improvement, for God's sake."

"Yes, sir. I'll be on point."

"You better be. Now get outta here."

Nate knew the berating wasn't over yet. He still had to make it through the locker room. As soon as he stepped in the door, someone sling-shot a jock strap into his chest.

"You suck, Camden!" someone yelled.

"Whassa matter? Is your bra too tight today?"

"Stay the hell offa the field, asshat!"

"The cheerleaders have an opening, you wuss!"

He felt a flash of anger, but stood silently taking it, Embrace the Suck.

Nate had been on the dishing side of this ritual many times but never on the receiving side. He knew enough to know it was best just to take it. Humiliation clogged the back of his throat like a piece of dry bread that wouldn't go down.

"Aren't black dudes supposed to be good at football?"

The room erupted in laughter. Nate felt his whole body lurch and adrenaline flooded his muscles. He clenched his fists and jaw to keep from fighting back. When the jeering finally quieted down he plopped in front of his locker, he cracked the knuckles on both hands.

His mind churned and whirled. Sophia was sick and missing. Had the mysterious visitors finally claimed a victim? He kept getting a mental picture of Sophia with her eyes plucked out leaving hollow black caverns. Had they come for her? Would it be over now? Would they come for each of them?

Nate shook his head to clear the thoughts. All he wanted now was to get his bike and go home. This suck was too big and too deep to embrace.

# CHAPTER NINETEEN

It had been cool during practice but now the wind picked up and it felt like the temperature was dropping. It had been so warm that morning he hadn't even worn a jacket; now he wished he had one. When he got to the bike rack he was surprised to see Missy waiting for him, but he was glad not to be walking by himself. She was on injured reserve but had stayed to watch cheer practice. It must have run long.

"Hi. Can we walk together?" Her voice sounded nasally.

"Yeah, sure. Hey, did you see Sophia today?"

Missy sniffled, "Only this morning when we got into a huge fight."

"A fight?"

"Nate, she's been talking stuff about me behind my back. Really mean stuff! She said I suck at cheering and that she was glad I got hurt because then she got to hang around you at the hospital."

"What? That doesn't sound like something she would say."

"Well, she did. And she said that I have-" her words got choked off by a fit of crying. "She said my hair is nappy! Can you believe it? She's not just a backstabber, but she's a racist bitch, too!"

Nate raised his eyebrows. Missy could have a mouth, but the b-word sounded strange coming out of her. Lindsey warned him cheerleading would corrupt Missy. He unlocked his bike and leaned it against the rack and gently put his hand on her good shoulder.

Leaning down to look her in the eye he said, "Missy, how do you know she said that? Did she say it to your face?"

"No, Kimberli told me."

"Uh-huh. Well, consider the source. I doubt if Sophia said any of that stuff."

"It wasn't just Kimberli! All the girls said they heard Sophia say it, too!"

"All the girls. Missy, those robots will do and say anything Kimberli tells them to. Let me show you something." He took his cell phone out and launched the confessions page and handed it to Missy.

She scrolled through screen after screen.

"What is this?" she asked.

"The school's confession page. All those posts about Sophia are by Kimberli and the other cheerleaders."

"Why? Why would they?"

"Because Kimberli is a psycho and jealous of Sophia."

"I didn't know anything about this stuff." She handed his phone back.

"Well, Sophia did. Her dad came into Ms. Garza's class looking for her. He said no one knows where she is and they can't find her."

"What?"

"She was going home sick. Probably after you guys got into a fight but when he got there she was gone and no one has seen her since. The worst part is that she's been seeing the same ghost kids that we did."

Missy twisted a strand of her long hair around her finger. "I'm sorry if she's having a hard time, but she brought it on herself. She's probably embarrassed that everyone knows the real Sophia now."

"Seriously? Did you hear anything I just said?"

"I heard you! It doesn't mean she didn't say all of those things. Come back here tonight to help set up for the carnival and you can ask Kimberli yourself."

"I have to come to set up the football booth anyway, but I'm not asking Kimberli what I already know."

"I can't believe you're taking Sophia's side. You're supposed to be my brother!"

"Whatever, Missy. Don't go all drama on me. Look, Ms. Kerpin is in a coma, you got hurt, and Sophia is missing because of the B-E-Ks! Don't you care?"

"B-E-Ks?"

"Garrett and I have been looking into it. Other people have seen them too, Missy. That's what they are called, Black Eyed Kids."

"You and Garrett? Have you lost it? I don't know what I saw that day. Even you said it was a prank. All I know is that this thing with Sophia is real and you don't care!" She snorted at him, turned on her heel and walked away.

Nate caught up with her and walked with his bike between them. Missy was still crying softly. That had not gone well. Seeing his sister cry, especially when it was his fault, made him feel small inside. He wanted to fix it for her, but he had no idea how.

This had been one of the worst days of his life. His pounding ego was now being echoed by a pounding headache. Nate wished they had never moved to this stupid development and changed schools. Then he never would have met Sophia or Kimberli and most of all he would never have seen the Black Eyed Kids. His whole world seemed foreign. He had always found comfort in his athletic ability. It allowed him to fit in anywhere, no matter what, even if his skin was a different color than most of his teammates. On the field, he always knew just what, when, and how to handle anything. After today, none of that mattered.

The icy silence continued when they walked in the door of the house. Missy stomped up the stairs and slammed her bedroom door. Nate dropped his stuff in the mudroom, and putting nothing away, he stomped his own way to the basement.

The workout room had only been used by Nate so far and that was just fine with him. The drywall that was cut away to remove the dead raccoon hadn't been repaired and cool air wafted from the space. He hadn't bothered to change out of his football pants and practice shirt, so all he had to do was get to it. With his earbuds securely placed in his ear, he cranked the music and loaded the barbell. It didn't take him long to get into his zone. Once he finished with the weights, he moved over to the treadmill. The rhythmic pounding of his feet in time with the music had a hypnotic effect on him. He felt sweat roll down his back and chest, and it made him feel powerful and in control. For the first time in weeks his mind was clear and his body was free.

He caught movement in his peripheral vision on the right side and almost stumbled when his heart jumped. Getting his balance back he looked toward the movement. His mom stood in the doorway with her hands on her hips.

He shut off the treadmill and yanked his earbuds out.

"I've been calling you for like ten minutes," she said.

"Sorry." He held up the earbuds in apology.

"What's up with Missy?"

"I dunno."

"She was slamming things around the living room. When I asked her what was wrong, she said to ask you."

Nate bit his lip. That little tattle-tale. "I dunno."

"Really?"

He couldn't resist that tone. "She's mad at me because I told her not to believe what some people say about other people at school."

"Who said what about whom?"

He cringed at her professional tone. He would not get out of this easily. Mel reached for a small towel on a stand near the door and tossed it to him. He sopped up his face and the back of his neck.

"Mom, if I tell you something can you keep it between us?"

"I'll try."

I'll try? What the hell did that mean?

"No, Mom. Seriously, I need to know it will stay between us."

She studied his face. He wasn't the little boy who took her word for gospel any more. Physically he had passed her up long ago but now he was becoming his own person with his own sense of things. As much as she wanted that it scared her a little.

"Nate, it depends on what you tell me. If someone is hurting themselves or others or plans to, I can't keep that to myself. Can you understand that?"

"I guess."

"If I can, I will keep it between us, OK?" She moved to sit on the weight bench.

Nate put the small towel on top of his head and Mel almost smiled, remembering when he was little and he carried his blankie around on his head. He sat crossed-leg in front of her on the floor.

"Some people at school have been bullying Sophia, and some rumors were started that caused a fight between her and Missy today."

"Bullying? But we live in a nice area. She's a nice girl, pretty, a cheerleader," Mel said.

Nate just about face-palmed himself, "Mom, bullying happens all the time. It doesn't matter who you are or what you do. You're either a bully or bullied." He winced inwardly at his experience earlier in the locker room.

"That's a depressing thought, Nate. What has been happening to Sophia and what about this fight?"

"It was just an argument over a rumor that Sophia said some stuff about Missy and her hair."

"Her hair? What about her hair?" The insurance fraud investigator was gone and now mama bear had shown up.

"Mom, it's not important! It's a big lie but Missy thinks it's true. Sophia may have taken off because of all the bullsh-" he caught himself, "stuff going on."

"Sophia wouldn't run off and not tell her dad just because of that."

He shrugged. He also knew there was a lot more going on. He couldn't tell her about the weird stuff, no way would she understand. He thought about the rumor that Sophia was a cutter, he thought about how she looked the day her mom had been at school, he thought about the weird stuff.

"It's pretty bad, Mom," he said, and he opened the confessions page on his phone and handed it to her.

He hadn't expected her to cry. She never cried. Twice in one day he had made the women he loved best cry.

"Who is posting this? Is it Missy?" she asked, shaking the phone at him.

"No. Missy didn't even know about it until I showed her."

"Then who?"

"I don't know."

Mel wiped at her cheeks. "Sophia and her dad have had a lot to deal with over the last few years. She needs friends. This is terrible. Nate, I have to tell her dad."

"Mom."

"It could help him find her. Maybe the police will do more than just take a runaway report from him. He's sick to death with worry, Nate."

He nodded. He knew how worried he felt; Mr. Lewis must feel a hundred times worse. Sophia could be in real trouble or worse. The mental picture of her with black shiny glass eyes pushed its way back into the forefront of his thoughts.

"OK," he said.

"I won't tell him how I found this terrible page, but it needs to be dealt with."

"OK." He wasn't sure exactly what she meant by dealt with but he was pretty sure it wouldn't be pleasant.

"Listen, I brought home some pizza. Go shower, let's eat and then head back over to school."

"What do you mean?"

"I volunteered to help set up for the carnival. I figured it was the least I could do with Ms. Kerpin being ill, and since you guys are going to be there anyway it seemed like a logical move."

The jolt of surprise forced a harsh laugh from his throat. This day had topped the list of firsts. First time he'd been heckled for his play, and the first time, ever, his mom had brought home pizza. His world was going crazy.

# CHAPTER TWENTY

The temperature continued to drop and by the time they got back to the school it started snowing microscopic flakes. It had been so warm only a few short hours ago that the snow was only making the roads wet. Soon it would be sticking to the grassy areas and weighing down the tree branches still heavy with colorful leaves.

Maybe it was the uncharacteristic pizza dinner, or Mel talking to her, but Missy's anger toward Nate had burned out. She was still giving him the silent treatment but it was fine, that would pass, too. He knew that Mel had passed the information on to Rick Lewis because he heard her on her cell phone before she closed the bedroom door.

Ms. Garza stood inside the doors directing people to where their group was setting up. Nate felt a small prickle as they passed through the door that had been replaced. He and Missy headed off to their areas, but his mom stayed and leaned in close to Ms. Garza. There was no doubt what they were talking about. The look on their faces said it all. Nate sighed. He felt a certain amount of relief having offloaded some of his burdens onto to people who could do something about it.

Right now he had to worry about facing his teammates again. The harassment wouldn't end until he redeemed himself on the field. Could his life suck any more right now?

He got the answer to that when he entered the gym where the team was supposed to set up their football toss. No one else was there. None of the stuff for the booth was anywhere to be seen. His phone vibrated, it was a picture of several of the team making an "L" shape with their index fingers and thumbs. Some were giving a single finger gesture. The message with it read: have fun loser!

Well, that explained why nobody else was here.

He heard a commotion behind him as more kids came into set up their carnival booths. Above the buzz, he could hear the unmistakable chatter of the cheerleaders.

"Hi Nate!" Kimberli called from across the room.

He didn't even turn to face them, but stood cracking his knuckles, trying to figure out what to do.

"Nate! I said hi," she shouted even louder.

He held his hand up but kept his back to her. It was bad enough being ditched by your team but did she have to bring attention to him?

"Yeah, Nate, she said hi," Lindsey giggled from behind him.

"Where is everybody?" Garrett's voice came from behind as well.

Of course, they were together.

Nate shrugged, "You know, typical jock idea of a joke."

Lindsey surveyed the empty area. "Ms. Garza told us to go find someone who might need help. You win!"

She flashed a smile at him, and he couldn't help but smile back.

"I don't even know where any of this junk is. We're just supposed to use the QB target net. It might be in the weight room."

"Well, you won't get any kids to come over if that's all you have. You need some bling," Lindsey said.

"Bling?"

"You know, decorations." She gestured with a sweeping arm for him to look around behind him. Other groups had helium balloons, streamers, and signs. He turned back to his empty space.

A static voice came from Garrett's back pocket. He pulled out one of the black walkie-talkies that staff used, "This is Garrett."

"Garrett, it's Ms. Garza. I need you in the cafeteria to help set up the sheeting for the pie throw. We need someone tall."

He grinned like the cat who swallowed the family goldfish. "On my way." Then to Nate and Lindsey, "Duty calls. I'll catch you guys later."

"What a nerd. That walkie-talkie has made him goofier than usual. I hope he doesn't go mad with power," Lindsey said. "Come on."

She grabbed Nate's hand and pulled him off towards the hallway. They'd have to scavenge materials for the booth. He trailed behind her and his nostrils filled with the scent of berries and vanilla. His stomach did that flip-flop thing again.

He didn't even think about Garrett until he heard a disapproving huff from the cheer booth as they walked past. He thought he should probably drop her hand but couldn't get his muscles to obey. Her fragrance seemed to have impaired his ability to focus. Lindsey walked with her shoulders back and her grip on his hand never wavered.

She went directly to a table in front of the library with a banner that read: Coding Club.

"Hey, guys. Do you think I could have some extra poster board?" she asked.

A boy with freckles across his nose looked from her to Nate.

"Oh, it's for me. Nate is just carrying everything," she smiled.

He smiled back, "Sure, whatever you need, Lindsey. Here take these markers, too."

She took the poster board and unopened box of markers and handed them to Nate.

"Thanks, guys! See you later." She spun on her heel and headed to her next stop.

Nate felt himself tighten. She headed for the Drama Club table. The kids in this club made him feel awkward. They liked to exchange lines from plays he had never heard of and then laugh when others around them didn't get it. They were loud and colorful and seemingly didn't care what anyone thought about it.

"Hi, Lindsey!" a tiny blonde hair girl waved from behind the table.

"What's wrong with Hannah?" Lindsey asked, gesturing to a red haired girl who was surrounded by other Drama Club kids.

"Oh. The cheerleaders made fun of the way she walks," she whispered.

Lindsey quickly moved around the table and enveloped Hannah in a bear hug. Nate stood alone on his side of the table feeling the blood rush to the top of his ears.

"What do they know? Bunch of stuck up nit-wits," Lindsey said.

"I can't help it. I'm not used to it yet. It's new. I outgrew the old one," Hannah sobbed.

Lindsey caught Nate's eye, and he grimaced. She lifted one of Hannah's pant legs a few inches. A shiny metal ankle rose up from her shoe.

"She was born without her foot," Lindsey said.

Nate tried not to look away. His grip tightened on the art supplies.

"It's OK, Hannah. When you're a famous actress you can trash them in your Academy Award speech," Lindsey said.

Hannah laughed. "I'll probably have forgotten all about them by then."

"That's right! Stupid hoes, what do they know? Hey, can I borrow some of those balloons?"

They visited several other booths and tables. Once Lindsey was satisfied they had enough stuff, they headed back toward the gym. Nate was disappointed that his hands were full this time. She looked back at him and a slight smile touched her lips as if she could read his thoughts. She studied him for a moment through the veil of black and peacock blue bangs that fell across her face.

He felt his face flush. She turned, continuing to lead the way. He couldn't keep his eyes from drifting down her back to her waist and curvy hips and the way they moved as she walked. For a minute he forgot where they were going. He jerked his head to the side to break his train of thought.

Down the darkened corridor he thought he saw a head with long dark hair peek out from a doorway and quickly disappear.

He stopped.

Lindsey turned around, "What's the matter?"

"I think I just saw Sophia." He headed toward what he thought he saw.

Lindsey struggled to keep up with his long strides. He burst into the doorway where he thought he saw Sophia. The room was dark, but he could see well enough to see it was empty.

"Are you sure?" Lindsey asked.

"No, I'm not sure. It may have just been the light. Come on, let's get this thing set up." He shrugged his shoulders to emphasize the stuff they had collected.

They hiked side-by-side down the corridor.

"She'll turn up, Nate. Everything probably just got to be too much for her. Garrett has texted her like 900 times every two minutes, but she hasn't texted back."

"It doesn't bug you if Garrett texts other girls?" He couldn't believe he just said that, maybe if there was a God, he only said it in his head.

She laughed. "Why would I care if Garrett texts other girls?"

"I don't know. I thought you guys were going out or something."

"My dad has known Garrett's dad since like Elementary school. Garrett and I have been friends since birth." She emphasized the word friends.

"Oh."

Lindsey smiled up at him and took some of the stuff out of his arms. His stomach responded with a flip-flop again as her hand brushed his chest.

They didn't waste any time and got right to work on the booth. When they finished, Nate had to admit that the football toss booth looked pretty great. Lindsey turned out to be an artist and created a professional looking poster to hang from the front of the table. The QB target was a tall structure with a net that had holes for targets; the idea was to throw the football through the hole. Colorful streamers cascaded from the top of the target net along with some balloons giving it a festive tone. The balloons didn't have any helium, but they still added the look of fun. Somewhere Lindsey came up with a laundry basket to hold the footballs. All they had to do now was clean up.

"Since when are you like on the football team?" Kimberli said to Lindsey as she slid up next to her.

"Jealous?" Lindsey quipped back.

"Right. You have the build for it, though." She turned her attention to Nate. "The booth looks good. Where is everyone else?"

"Thanks, but Lindsey did it. I don't know where they are, exactly."

"Ah, sweet little Linds, always ready to like help out. By the way, where's Garrett?" Kimberli said.

Nate glared at her. "Can we do something for you?"

"No. I just wanted to tell you, and your teammates, of course, that I'll have like some schnapps at the carnival tomorrow."

"Why?" Nate asked.

"Why? Why not. Why should the little kids like have all the fun," Kimberli said. "I'm totally willing to share."

"Share your expulsion, that is," Lindsey said. "Where do you plan on getting it?"

"From Mom and Daddy, of course."

"Don't call him that. It's weird," Lindsey said.

Kimberli opened her mouth to reply and Nate was ready to unleash on her for being a liar and crappy to Lindsey and messing with his sister's head and picking on a girl who had no foot, but Garrett entered the gym and cut him off.

"Hey guys, Ms. Garza says five minutes and then we gotta get outta here!"

Missy came over with Kimberli's purse and jacket. "Here's your stuff."

"Thanks. Did you finish what I told you to?"

"Yeah, we're all ready for tomorrow."

"Good."

"Minion training is coming along well, I see," Lindsey said.

Missy narrowed her eyes at Lindsey but kept quiet.

"Oh Linds, your ability to be like nerdy and clueless always exceeds my expectations," Kimberli said.

Several rows of lights in the gym powered down with a loud noise, leaving widely separated spotlights from the rows still on. Taking the hint, kids started filing out in a noisy cluster.

"Do you guys need any help?" Garrett asked.

"Nah, we got it. We're done," Nate said.

Much to Nate's annoyance, Kimberli walked out with them. His anger toward her built with every step. If Missy didn't see her for what she was, she'd be doing more than delivering Kimberli's purse. In his head, he was playing out what he needed to say to Kimberli.

The shadows in the gym had grown long, and the abandoned gaiety of the booths seemed lonely. They were the last group to leave. Nate was debating if he should start in on Kimberli before they left the gym or after. They were almost to the door when a huge bang behind them stopped them in their tracks. Everyone jumped, but Kimberli was the only one to spin back. Missy reached out and clutched Nate's sleeve.

He turned slowly toward the sound.

Standing just out of the shadow in a pool of light was a slight figure. Kimberli clicked her tongue. Nate breathed out a sigh of relief.

"Sophia!" Garrett said and rushed toward her. "Where the hell have you been? Your dad and everyone has been looking for you."

As he approached, she stepped back keeping distance between them.

Nate pulled out his cell and texted his mom: Sophia is here

Garrett ducked as the bulb in the light directly above Sophia exploded in a burst of sparks and smoke. Before he could gather himself, several other lights followed suit leaving the gym in near total darkness. Garrett rushed forward and struggled against the blackness to see. The space where Sophia had been was empty.

The door behind them clanged open and Missy let out a scream. Mel and Linda rushed through the door.

"What happened? Where is she?" Linda asked.

"The lights just like blew up!" Kimberli said.

"Where is Sophia?" Mel asked.

"She was right here but when the lights went out she took off." Garrett held his hands out as if he had dropped a priceless vase. She had disappeared into thin air, but how else could he explain it?

"Did she say something? Did you say something?" Linda asked.

"No, she just stood there," Nate said.

"OK. I'm calling her Dad," Mel said.

Linda phoned Mr. Greene, and he showed up wearing sweat pants, brown snow boots, and a hat that made him look like a snowman. When Mr. Lewis arrived, he immediately searched the gym. Mr. Greene made sure all the kids were gone and then he phoned the police and district security. Mel helped search the locker room and all the girl's bathrooms on the main floor. Nate and Missy waited for her in the main office; Mr. Greene didn't feel their help was appropriate. There was no sign of Sophia.

"Come on guys. The police will check the building and grounds more carefully," Mel said.

"Hey, kids?" a heavy set man in a district security uniform approached them.

Mel placed a protective hand on each of their shoulders.

"I'm Officer Baldwin. Can you guys think of any place Sophia might go? Like the house of a friend her Dad doesn't know about?" He peered at them over thin-wired eyeglasses.

"No," Nate answered.

"How about you, miss?" he asked Missy.

"No. She's always home, here, or at dance. No secret boyfriend or anything," Missy answered.

He placed his hands on his hips and the leather gun belt creaked. "All right. Well, if she contacts you let your folks know right away. It's not safe for a young girl to wander around at night. As her friends, I'm sure you want her home safe, too."

"Of course. Thank you, Officer," Mel said and she ushered her kids out the door.

The snow had gotten serious while they were inside. It was a heavy wet snow that made the once warm sidewalks and roads slushy. The temperature had plummeted and Nate saw the slush was turning icy in spots. He pulled the hood up on his sweatshirt.

As Mel warmed up the car Nate used the brush to get the snow off the windows. He had to scrape thick ice off the windshield and his hands were freezing and his socks were sloshing in his shoes by the time he finished. Even though the car was a small hybrid sedan he had to lean against it to reach the middle part of the windshield and the front of him was soaked.

"They didn't say anything about it being this bad of a storm," Mel said as he got into the passenger seat.

"Maybe they'll cancel the football game tomorrow?" Missy asked from the backseat.

Nate huffed. "I doubt it. I guess if the roads are too bad for the other team's bus to get here, but otherwise, we play." He had to play.

They were the only car on the road. The snow was falling in big chunky flakes that had a disorienting effect as they came at the windshield. Even set on high, the wiper blades were having a hard time keeping up with the snow. The headlights, too, seemed to have a difficult time penetrating the storm. Mel was driving a considerable amount below the speed limit, but the car still slid on the ice. The thump-thump of the windshield wipers and the warmth of the heater made Nate realize how tired he was.

"Mom, do you think Sophia will be OK?" Missy asked in a hesitant voice.

"I think so. She'll come home and everything will be fine," Mel answered. "I'm sure you guys can work out whatever has happened between you."

As they approached the last main intersection before home, Nate noticed a group of three kids standing with their heads hunkered down against the storm in the pool of light cast by the only street light on the darkened stretch of road.

"Why are those kids out in the storm?" Mel asked.

They had a green light and Mel continued to go through the intersection at that same steady speed she had been driving.

The tallest boy under the streetlight looked up and right at them. Just as it registered that he had black soulless eyes, insect eyes, Mel sucked in a shocked breath causing Nate to turn towards her. He couldn't see her face though because all he saw was the blinding headlights of another car headed right at them.

Exploding airbags and metal twisting metal should have drowned out every other sound but all he could hear was Missy.

"Mom! Mom! Mom!" she cried over and over.

When everything came to a stop, he moved his head back to Mel's direction, and glass shards tumbled out of his hair and down the front of his clothes. The white side curtain airbag was where the window should have been. It blocked his view of what hit them. The windshield wipers were still steadily thumping away as if nothing had happened.

"Mom?" he asked.

"Is everyone OK?" she shouted in a voice fueled by adrenaline.

"I think so, " Nate said as calmly as he could.

"My shoulder, Mom! My shoulder!" Missy cried.

Nate started when someone banged on his window. Ms. Garza's very concerned face filled the space. She pulled his door open and more glass spilled out onto the road.

"We're OK. We're OK. We're OK," Mel chanted.

"Mrs. Camden, can you climb over and come out Nate's side?" Ms. Garza asked.

Mel stopped her chant and moved toward Linda and let out a shriek. "I think my arm is broken!"

"Mooom!" Missy cried.

Nate got out and Linda got in. She leaned across the center console and rubbed Mel's good arm and spoke to her in a low, soothing tone. Nate yanked Missy's door open and sank to the seat next to her. He put his arm around her shoulders. Missy was stiff as a board at first but melted under the warmth of his arm and pressed into him. He could hear sirens approaching.

"Mrs. Camden, you might be in shock. Help is on the way, you're going to be all right," Linda said.

The inside of the car lit up with blue and red lights. A policeman put his hand on top of the car and leaned in Linda's open door.

"Everyone OK?"

"No, they're going to need an ambulance," Linda said.

"Can anyone tell me what happened?" he asked.

Nate was doing his best to keep it together but what he heard next almost broke his resolve.

In a hysterically high voice Mel answered, "Oh God, I don't think they were human."

# CHAPTER TWENTY-ONE

The policeman took a statement from Nate and one from Linda. Nate's was short considering he hadn't seen much. Linda had been right behind them and saw the whole thing. She told the policeman that the other car was traveling too fast for the conditions and couldn't stop for the red light. The SUV sailed right through the intersection and broadsided the Camdens' car. She didn't mention seeing any kids. Nate didn't either.

Mel, Missy, and the other driver had been taken to the hospital by ambulance. It had taken some effort to get Mel out of the car. Linda and Nate sat on the back running board of the fire engine and Linda dialed the number Nate gave her for David. As she told him the situation, Nate shivered against the cold. She handed the phone to Nate when all the important details had been told.

"Dad?"

"Yeah, buddy. Are you all right?"

"I guess. Mom's car is legit jacked. They'll have to tow it."

"It's OK. I don't care about the car. Ms. Garza is going to drive you to the hospital, all right? I'll meet you there."

"OK."

He lumbered over to Linda's happy yellow VW bug. He wasn't sure it would make it through the snow. A yellow daisy rested in the built-in flower vase on the dash. He almost laughed. The whole thing was so inappropriately happy it was absurd. He slammed the door shut and closed his eyes, struggling to keep himself together.

The driver's side door opened with a sucking sound and cold air swirled around him. It stopped snowing, but the wind picked up and blew the flakes in wild patterns.

They rode in silence, the little car bucking at the snow.

David was waiting for them at the ER entrance. Mel and Missy were both in X-ray and Linda made sure that David insist that Nate be seen. The paramedic at the scene had cleared him, but she thought he might be in shock or something. The flying glass left several marks on his face and his demeanor troubled her.

Linda went up to Inna's room after Nate went back to be examined. Ben was sleeping in what looked to be an uncomfortable slouch in the chair. A heart monitor beeped quietly but steadily. The respirator hissed a fretful rhythm. Linda touched Inna's hand. It was warm but motionless. A feeling of vulnerability overwhelmed her. No place on this earth was safe from tragedy.

She left the room after leaving a note for Ben. He didn't wake up when she slipped it onto the arm of the chair. He snored softly in unison with the machine breathing for Inna.

Linda found David and Nate sitting in a family waiting area. Nate slumped in his chair, his dark hair still wet from the snow. His hands on his knees were clenched into fists.

"Hi, guys. How's it going?" she asked.

"The other guy is OK, broken nose from his airbag. Mel has a broken arm and they are setting it right now. They want to do an MRI because they think she may have a head injury. Missy is fine. The crash didn't cause any more damage to her shoulder. She's just going to be sore," David said.

"And Nate, are you all right?" Linda asked.

He nodded, his head never looking up. He grabbed an open soda from the table in front of him and held it between his knees.

"The doc looked at him and other than a few minor cuts on his face from the window he's fine," David answered for him.

"This hospital is becoming an unwelcome second home for us," she said to Nate. "Is Mrs. Camden going to be all right?" she asked.

"I think so. She's a little confused right now. She thinks some kids on the roadside caused the accident. No one knows what she is talking about."

"Kids? I didn't see anyone out there, but she did say some odd things."

"Yeah, that's why they think she bumped her head." David pinched the bridge of his nose.

Nate's head popped up. "You didn't see anyone?"

"No, but it was snowing pretty hard and my eyes were glued to the road. Did you see some kids?"

"Maybe," he mumbled and brought the pop to his mouth and guzzled.

"Anyway, thank you for stopping," David said.

"Of course. I'm glad I could help. Nate was very calm through the whole thing; you should be very proud of him."

Nate let his pop can slip from his hands and it clanged to the floor, the sound echoing off the walls. He buried his face in hands and sobbed. David looked like someone had slapped him across the face and no one moved or spoke for several seconds.

David rose slowly and went to the chair next to his son and put his arm around him and squeezed. Nate buried his face into his dad's chest and any resolve he had to keep it together dissolved.

Linda silently slipped from the room to leave them to their privacy.

## CHAPTER TWENTY-TWO

Linda's house was in the Dark Pine Hills development and she didn't have too far to drive. She knew it might not be the best idea to live in the same place that she taught, but she had fallen in love with the area. Her house was in the small patio home area of the subdivision.

Each of the four alcoves of four homes shared outside spaces and a hot tub area. Her neighbors were mostly older folks tired of the upkeep of lawns and downsizing in the absence of raising children. A few lots were in various stages of renewed building. Her place was finished and fully landscaped when she bought it. The original buyers had only lived there for a few months when the husband suffered a stroke and passed away. The wife sold to Linda for slightly below market so she could move back to California to be closer to family.

The wind picked up and plastic sheeting and other construction materials from nearby lots flapped and banged, giving her the false sense of someone moving around in the shadows. The icy sidewalk dashed any ideas she had of taking a soak in the hot tub. A hot bath would have to do. She didn't turn on any lights as she made her way through the house to her master suite.

The master bathroom had sold her on the place. It was huge and felt like her a private spa featuring a shower with numerous heads and a deep, glorious soaker tub. She cranked the hot water and streamed some sweet-smelling bath oil under the faucet of the tub. As the tub filled she started soft music in the entertainment center in the bedroom so it would pipe peacefully through the speakers in the bathroom. She stood in the mirror and pulled her hair up loosely into a clip. The sound of tapping on the front door made her stop and listen.

Tinkling of water into the tub, the music, nothing else. Probably just the wind.

The warm and fragrant water of the bath felt like a hug as she slid in up to her ears. She put a washcloth over her face and tried to concentrate on the sultry sounds floating through the speaker above the tub, but unwanted thoughts kept creeping in.

She saw Inna, lying motionless in her hospital bed. The bed morphed into a silk-lined casket, but Inna's face and position never changed. She saw Sophia huddled against the snow, then running out into the road, almost being hit by Mel Camden's car. Nate hanging out of the driver's side window, sobbing tears of blood. The scene played out again, but this time, she saw Sophia being hit by the car and tossed to the side of the road. Snow was quickly covering her motionless body, cars passing and never seeing her.

Next, Sophia cowering in a dark corner while the hands of a madman grabbed for her.

That scene faded into a new horror. Sophia suspended by her neck in that dark corner with ghostly hands of children grabbing at her legs, pulling her against the noose, her tongue lolling obscenely from her mouth.

Linda sat bolt upright and sucked her breath in, bringing bath water into her lungs. She flung herself, coughing and sputtering over the side of the tub, splashing water onto the floor. Her heart was banging dangerously hard in her chest and she struggled to suck air into her lungs. She coughed so hard she thought she would throw up. Forcing her throat and lungs open, she made a terrible wheezing sound. After several long minutes, she could move air normally again. Without bothering to drain the tub, she wrapped herself tightly in a thick cotton robe and put on thick socks. She felt chilled to the bone.

She started the electric kettle in the kitchen to make some hot tea. That's when she heard it, a faint knock on the door. She turned the kettle off and listened. This time a little louder, three knocks on the front door.

*Definitely not the wind.*

She crept through the long dark entry hall and pushed herself up to the peephole. No one. Looking as wide as the peephole would let her all she saw was the dark, icy night.

Going back to the kitchen, she resumed her tea making. She went into the bedroom and turned off the music. The chatter of the television is what she needed right now. Linda was about to press the on button on the remote when the doorbell rang. She jumped and dropped the remote. It crashed to the hardwood floor, its back came off and the batteries rolled away.

Her nerves buzzed as she made her way back to the front door. No one ever came to her door. If it was those damn kids, they were in for a rude awakening. She wanted lights on, but the concealment of the dark seemed prudent. She peered out the peephole. This time, she saw the back of a head. A man's head covered with a familiar Colorado University Buffaloes winter hat. Adrenaline surged through her like an electric shock. Her first instinct was to pretend not to be home. The doorbell rang again.

Without warning, her initial shock gave way to a red-hot anger. She yanked the door open.

"Josh! What are you doing here?" she demanded.

"Lin, I just have to talk to you," he said.

"How did you find me?"

"The internet." He shrugged.

"Uh, I don't even care how. You need to leave right now."

"Please, Lin. Just two seconds. Come on. I drove all the way down here in the storm. Please, Lin."

He looked pathetic. Handsome, but pathetic. She bit the inside of her cheek, indecision gripping her.

"Please, Lin. Just give me two seconds. If you never want to talk to me again after that, I'll leave."

"I-"

"Come on, Lin. It's freezing out here."

"Two minutes, Josh. That's it." She opened the door wider and stood aside.

He stomped the snow off his shoes and brushed past her.

"Wow, this is a nice place. You did good."

"Hmm, you're two minutes starts now."

"Can't I even sit down first?"

She sighed. "Whatever," and led the way down the entry hall to the living room.

She noticed that he hadn't taken off his shoes and had tracked snow all the way down the hall and onto the delicate floral print carpet under his feet. The familiar twinge of annoyance jumped up in her.

"Well, time's a wasting, Josh."

"Look, Lin. I hate the way things ended between us. I always felt we could work it out, but you left before we even had a chance."

"What? Who wanted to go to counseling?"

"I know. But I thought we could do it on our own. Obviously, I was wrong."

Her heart softened. It was the first time he had said he was wrong that she felt he meant it.

"I never stopped loving you. At the very least, I hope that we can be friends, stay in touch. I really care about you," he said.

Tears touched her lids.

"It was never that I didn't love you, Josh. You-I needed understanding and support."

"I know. I messed up. I was selfish. I'm sorry."

"Well, I accept your apology."

He smiled. "Fantastic! As my first act of being a friend, tell me how things are going?"

"I never said we could be friends."

"Come on, Linda."

She sighed. "Well, I love my new school. It's brand new and gorgeous. My principal is kind of a jerk but the rest of the staff is great. It's so different from where I was before."

"That's great, Linda. I'm really happy for you that you're back at work."

"Thanks, it feels good. My good friend that teaches next door has been sick in the hospital, so that sucks."

"Oh, I'm sorry. Is he going to be all right?"

She snickered. "It's a she and we don't know if she'll be OK. It's pretty serious."

"Oh, that does suck. She's lucky to have you as a friend."

"Thanks for saying that."

"This really is a nice place. I saw the sign at the front of the development, from the low $600's. Pricey area must be lots of wealthier families."

"Yeah, I guess so. Some of the families were here before the housing crash, so I doubt they paid that much. I certainly didn't."

"Well, less poverty, less problems."

"No, just different ones, I guess."

"Really? How are the students?"

"Hmm, well, one of my students ran away from home today and I found out the kids have been posting horrible things about each other on a secret website. I just came from taking a student to the ER after a car accident. But other than that they are great."

"You took him to the ER?"

"Yeah, I was right behind them when it happened."

"But why did you take the student? Isn't that beyond your job description?"

She stared at him. "Are you kidding me? Back to that same crap? What happened to 'I was selfish'?"

"What do you mean? The bigger problem was and still is that your students mean more to you than anything, including me. You still aren't able to differentiate between your job and your life."

"No, Josh. The problem has always been that you couldn't accept that my job is my life. You just aren't mature enough to accept that my world did not revolve around you. Thank God we never had children!"

"Wow, Linda, that's hitting below the belt. I always wanted children, but it was never the right time for you!"

"You know what? This is fruitless. Your two minutes are up." She stood up.

"Wait, wait, Linda. This is why we should go to counseling."

"Counseling? Why? So you can try and fix me? You clearly don't believe that you have done anything wrong. Please leave."

He didn't move. "Come on, Linda. Let's start over. This conversation's gone all wrong."

"Get out of my house. If I have to call the cops, Josh, I will."

He stood up and held his hands out to her, "OK, OK, calm down."

"Get out! If you show up here or call me again I swear I will file for harassment with the police!"

"Same old drama queen. What the hell was I thinking?" He turned and stomped to the door. He shut it with such force the candle holder on the wall next to it crashed to the floor.

She went into the den that had the lone window facing the street and watched him gun his car down the slippery road. Why had she let him in? She knew it wouldn't go well. Tears of frustration welled in her eyes.

She ditched the tea and poured herself a glass of red wine. The alcohol warmed and loosened her tight muscles. She put the batteries back in the remote and turned the television on, but she wasn't watching the drama that played across the screen. There was enough drama in her life. The wine made her body feel heavy. She was thinking about heading to bed when she thought she heard a knock at the front door again.

She muted the television.

A slight rapping.

Josh must have come back. She stormed to the front door armed with her cell phone. Dialing 9-1-1 and keeping her finger on the send button she peeked out the peephole. There were two kids hunched against the cold under hoodies. Their faces hidden by the hoods.

"Who is it?" she called through the closed door.

"We're lost. Can we come in and use your phone?"

"Don't you have a cell phone?"

"No, ma'am."

"Well, give me the number you need and I'll call for you."

"It's very cold out here."

"OK, I'll call whoever you want."

"Please, can we come in?"

Understanding spread through her brain. It's the kids. The kids with black eyes. Fear shot through her veins.

"Who are you? Show me your faces!"

"Let us in. It won't take long."

"I said who are you?"

The taller of two turned his face up to the peephole. There were no whites of his eyes, no iris, no pupil, just damp blackness. He smiled. It was like watching an alligator open its jaws for the kill.

"Oh! Dios Mio!" she breathed.

"Please, we need to come in," he said.

She pressed send.

# CHAPTER TWENTY-THREE

It wasn't a surprise that the police couldn't find anyone. Inna and Mel both said the same thing. *They weren't human.* Looking into its eyes, she knew it was true.

After the responding officer assured her that everything looked to be in order, she spent the rest of the night on the couch. Every light in the house blazed, and she clutched a long handled barbecue fork to her chest. She must have fallen asleep somewhere along the line because her buzzing cell phone woke her. The barbecue fork still clenched to her chest, her entire body protested letting it go.

She groped for her phone.

"Hello?"

"Hi, Ms. Garza. Sorry to bother you at home." It was David Camden.

"Oh, Mr. Camden. Is everything all right?"

"Yes, I just wanted to thank you again for your help last night."

"It's no problem, really. How is everyone today?"

"Good. I got everyone home early this morning. Nate's too sore to play in the football game today but he and Missy will be at the carnival this evening. I understand Mel is supposed to man the snack table?"

"Um, I think so, but if she's not up to it that's completely understandable."

"Uh, no. She said to tell you that she will be there. They determined that she didn't have a concussion. I guess she was just confused or something. She does have a cast on her left arm, so I'll be coming to help her."

"That's perfect, Mr. Camden."

"OK, great. See you later then?"

"Of course. Mr. Camden?"

"Yeah?"

"It's possible that your wife did see some kids last night."

"Oh." He sounded less than enthusiastic.

"I mean she probably did see them and didn't hit her head, just so you know." Shut up, her mind screamed at her.

"Yeah, ok. Thanks. See you later this evening." She cringed at his tone.

Relieved to hang up, she checked the time on her phone. It was already 10:30, she was surprised she had slept so late. The house was quiet around her, streams of sunlight warmed the room. The memory of last night pounced on her.

Something sinister was happening. It was as if an onerous darkness had boiled up from the earth and blanketed them, bringing these creatures with it. She caught sight of the dark woods beyond her backyard through the window. Maybe it had seeped out of there. The story of the haunted cave entered her mind. Maybe Inna was right. If these dark things were possible, didn't it mean God was too? She didn't comprehend what these beings were or where they came from, but she wasn't taking any chances.

Before she got in the shower, she opened the ornate jewelry box on her dresser. She lifted a delicate golden cross and chain out of the velvet lined box. It glinted happily in the late morning sun. Fastening it around her neck, she felt disappointed that her feelings of dread were still with her.

\*\*\*

"Was that Ms. Garza?" Nate asked when David hung up the phone on the kitchen wall.

"Yes."

"Dad?"

"Yeah?"

"I saw some kids standing by the side of the road when we had our accident."

"Hmm. Yeah, Ms. Garza said the same thing. Well, kids didn't cause the wreck. A guy driving too fast for the conditions did. They probably took off when the crash happened. Don't worry about it, son."

He couldn't help but worry. Had Ms. Garza seen them?

Missy was propped up on the couch with pillows watching television. She had a large blue ice pack on her shoulder. Mel hadn't been down yet.

Last night when Mel finished getting her arm set at the hospital and came into the waiting area he had still been crying. She didn't say one word but had hugged him with her good arm and cuddled him to herself. David ushered them all to his car when Missy joined them. Mel walked next to Nate, stretching to keep her arm around his shoulders. Her coat half on, one shoulder draped over her casted arm, and it occurred to him he should be escorting her. David pushed Missy out in a wheelchair. It had been a silent ride home.

Nate sat down in the armchair across from Missy and winced. His neck and shoulders were tight and sore. The ER doctor said he was fine but should take a break from football for the next couple of days. That meant he wouldn't be able to squelch the bullying for now. Only a good game would do that or some unlucky person to play worse than he had and shift the focus off of him.

David rushed around the kitchen, preparing a tray to take to Mel.

"Nate? Did Mom see the ghost kids, too?" Missy whispered.

"I think so."

"What does it mean?"

"I don't know. I really don't."

"Coach Summers says he still would like you to come be on the sidelines today, if you feel up to it," David called from the kitchen.

No. He didn't.

"Nate, it's my fault that Sophia is missing," Missy said, tears were glistening on her cheeks.

"It's not your fault, Missy. Don't cry. It's all going to be OK." He hated it when she cried.

"We need to tell Dad or a priest or somebody. I think our neighborhood needs an exorcism," she said.

He laughed.

"No, Nate! I'm serious!"

"I know. I'm sorry. I didn't mean to laugh, but this whole situation is insane. Maybe. I don't even know where to find a priest, do you?"

"We could look online."

"Yeah, maybe. I'm not sure if it works that way. I should go get dressed."

"I could come sit the bench with you. I'm benched too," she said.

He stretched his neck to each side. "Yeah, that'd be fine. Just stay away from Dillon, OK."

"Dillon? No problem. He's a Neanderthal." She didn't really want to go. Missy didn't want to see her squad perform without her, but it seemed like Nate needed somebody to watch his back.

Mel was not thrilled with Missy going to the football game, but David convinced her it would do the kids good to get out. He'd make sure she dressed warmly. They would be right at the school and he and Mel could meet up with them before the carnival started. Nate wasn't sure if any of it was a good idea. But these things could show up at home just as easily as anywhere else, so what did it matter? He shoved his hands in his hoodie pocket and clenched the small silver medal hidden in there. He trudged up the stairs to get dressed.

When they left the house to get in David's car, it seemed to Nate as if the seasons changed overnight. Today the sun was bright, and the temperature already warm enough that the snow was beginning to melt. The field would be a soggy mess and Nate was incredibly disappointed that he couldn't play. He had never missed a game before and soggy fields were the best.

When they got to the game, Coach Summers seemed sympathetic to his plight. He let Missy come and stand on the sideline with Nate. She grabbed a blanket on the way out of the house and had it draped around her shoulders, but she stayed glued to Nate's side. The guys' focus was on the game and no one gave him any of the crap he expected. He and Missy stayed far to one end to avoid too much interaction, in case their focus shifted. Nate noticed that Missy kept looking at the cheerleaders.

"That kid Eric that's in my position today is pretty good," he said.

"He's OK. He has terrible body control, though. Totally not aware of where his feet are. On that last pass he should have realized that he was going to step out of bounds and dragged his back foot, like I've seen you do," she said.

"You noticed?"

"Nate, I've been watching you play football as long as I can remember. Of course I noticed."

His phone buzzed in his back pocket.

*Group text message: Watch your back Camden. Eric is coming for your spot.*

So much for no crap. While he contemplated a comeback, a new message arrived.

*Lindsey: Hey how come you are not playing?*

*Nate: Fender bender last night. I'm not cleared to play.*

*Lindsey: Are you OK*

*Nate: Yes. Just sore*

*Lindsey: well crap I only came here to see you play*

*Nate: you're here?*

*Lindsey: behind you*

Nate turned around. Lindsey and Garrett were in the first bleacher waving at him. He waved back.

"She's pretty," Missy said.

"You think?" Nate grinned.

"Oh my God. You are such a nerd," she laughed.

It was good to hear her laugh. He laughed with her.

Half-time hit and Nate left Missy to go with the team into the locker room. The cheer squad took the field for their half-time performance. Missy stood by herself looking like a small child who had not been invited to play at the playground.

"Missy! Missy!" Lindsey called. She patted the blanketed bench seat next to her.

Missy wandered up to the bleachers and sat down.

"I'm Lindsey, do you know Garrett?"

"Hi," Missy said.

"Ladies and Gentlemen, the Dark Pine Grizzly Cheerleading Squad!" came over the loudspeakers.

The music started and Missy turned her attention to the performance. They were missing two bodies, and the routine looked a little out of sync, but still good. Missy wasn't sure if she should be happy about that.

"I bet they'll be glad when you can come back," Lindsey said.

"Maybe. I think they're looking for a replacement. I might be able to come back by basketball season but I will miss all the competitions before that. So I might just end up a sidelines cheerleader."

"Don't worry about it. I know that Kimberli is kind of freaking out because they need your tumbling skills."

"How do you know that?"

"I heard her talking to her mom about it this morning."

Missy raised her eyebrows.

"I have to live with her. I'm Kimberli's stepsister."

"Oh. I didn't know she had a stepsister."

Lindsey laughed. "Yeah, well she would prefer that no one knew. I'm not exactly her dream sister, if you know what I mean."

Missy studied her for a second. Her blue hair and nose piercing said edgy but there seemed more to her than that. If Nate liked her, there must be. The two stepsisters were seemingly trying to be exact opposites.

They cheered along with the rest of the crowd when the teams took the field again. Nate came up to the bleachers instead of staying on the sidelines.

"You OK?" Missy asked.

"My neck is just so tight. I've got a headache coming."

Garrett scooted over and made room for him next to Lindsey. Nate dug a couple of aspirins from his pocket and dry swallowed them. The heat of the sun on his back loosened his stressed muscles. Lindsey reached behind him and rubbed his shoulders. He felt a deeper warmth than the sun.

Maybe this was a respite before the next terrible thing happened but for now Nate relaxed. All he could do was wait and see and hope everything would work itself out somehow. He couldn't bring himself to tell Garrett and Lindsey about last night. Garrett was trying so hard to convince himself that it was over, Nate couldn't bear to squash his hope.

Nate had been wrong about Eric. He was good but had no stamina. The second half had been dismal, and his team lost by fourteen painful and unanswered points. The one good thing about the loss was maybe now the focus would be off Nate. Besides, he only had one bad practice; it wasn't like he cost them a win or anything.

His parents met them after the game and they went out for dinner before going back to school for the carnival. They drove a little way into Littleton, just north of their development, to go to Mel's favorite restaurant. Having her dominant left hand in a cast made eating a little tricky for Mel, but she tried to make light of it. Nate kept watching her during dinner. She seemed a little tired but not overly distraught. Like him after the encounter on the front porch, she was in that early stage of convincing herself that there was a logical explanation for what she had seen the night of the accident.

They got back to school earlier than planned. The kids stuck around and helped Mel and David set up the snack table. She assured them she was fine but stood back and let them do most of the work. When they were done, Missy and Nate went off to find their groups and get their booths ready for visitors. With so many people around, Nate hoped things would go well, although these creatures didn't seem to mind a crowd. That's how he began thinking of them, creatures.

"Hey, Nate?" Missy grabbed his hand before they went into the gym.

"Yeah?"

"Do you think Kimberli really will have alcohol?" she whispered.

"I don't know. Don't worry about her, all right. If it's weird just tell them your shoulder hurts and go find mom, OK?"

"Yeah," she squeezed his hand and bounced into the gym ahead of him.

Bryce was alone at the football booth. He texted furiously on his phone. Nate shored himself up and headed that way. Embrace the Suck.

"Hi Nate," he said when he looked up.

"Hey. Tough game today."

"Don't remind me. It sucks to suck. Are you going to be OK to play next week?"

"Yeah, I should be."

"Thank God. These other clowns are worthless."

"Worthless? Who is? Nate?" Dillon punched Nate in the arm as he entered the booth.

"Oww!"

"Hey jackwagon, he was in a car wreck yesterday," Bryce said.

"Oh man, I'm sorry. I spaced it," he said and held his hands up in surrender.

"No problem," Nate said.

"The booth looks good. Sorry about that," Bryce said.

"It's cool, I got some help."

Lindsey stood by the entrance to the gym. She waved to Nate when he looked her way.

"Well, who couldn't use that kind of help," Dillon said, he held invisible large breasts in front of him and pretended to juggle them.

Nate thought about punching him in the face, but a group of younger kids pushed around Lindsey in a noisy group. The doors must have opened to the first group of kids. They streamed every which way, but a large group of them beelined it to the Quarterback Toss booth.

"Here we go," Bryce smiled.

Their booth was busy with a steady stream of kids. Other players drifted in and out, but Bryce and Nate stayed the whole time. He noticed that when boys left the booth they were all heading toward the weight room instead of other booths in the gym or out to the other areas of the school that were being used for the carnival. Then he noticed Kimberli and another girl coming out of the weight room, giggling. She must have really brought it.

Nate looked over to the hugging booth to check on Missy. She looked awkward hugging Dillon with her one good arm and he looked like he wouldn't let her go anytime soon. Now Nate really wanted to punch him in the face. Garrett appeared behind Dillon and tapped his shoulder. There was a brief exchange between the two of them that ended with Dillon leaving. Garrett stepped up and gave Missy a quick hug. He looked over to Nate and gave a thumbs up.

"I told you he was a nerd." Lindsey had come to stand next to him without him noticing.

She wore a loose flowing peacock blue shirt, dark jeans, and brown boots. She didn't have any makeup on that he could tell, but she looked like she could pose for a magazine. He was thinking the sight of her was making him hallucinate because she smelled delicious.

"I've been making cotton candy with your dad." She held up her hand to show him the sticky sugary spiderweb between her fingers.

"Yum. That must have been fun."

She looked past him. "That can't be good," she said gesturing toward the crowd.

It took Nate a few seconds of scanning in the direction she had indicated to find Missy. Her mouth drawn down in a frown and she leaned back against the direction of travel. Kimberli led her by the wrist in the direction of the weight room.

"Oh, man. Hey Bryce, I gotta go for sec. I'll be right back," Nate said.

"Sure."

Lindsey and Nate made their way through the crowded gym to the weight room. In between rounds, Kimberli's bottle was being stashed in a small rolled up mat in the corner of the room. Kids were passing it around a nervous circle. Missy was next.

"I don't think I should. I mean I'm taking painkillers for my shoulder. I don't think I should mix them," she said.

"I thought you were like more mature than most seventh graders, Missy," Kimberli said.

"If she doesn't want to leave her alone," Lindsey said.

"Of course she wants to," Kimberli said. "Don't you?" She held the bottle out to Nate.

The other kids stared.

"Don't be a wuss." It was Eric from the back of the circle.

"Come on, Missy," Nate said.

Someone clucked like a chicken.

"Now we know why you suck at football, no balls," Eric said.

The group laughed. Anger burned in Nate's throat. He swiped the bottle from Kimberli's hand.

"Nate, don't," Lindsey said.

He tipped it back and took a long swig. The heavy peppermint burned like fire down his throat igniting an explosion in his gut.

Kimberli grinned. "See Lindsey, it's easy."

The door opened and they all jumped. Garrett slipped in.

"What are you guys doing?" Then he saw the bottle. "Ooooh."

"I'm just trying to make a man like out of Lindsey," Kimberli said. "She has a mannish haircut, so we're like off to good start."

The group laughed. Lindsey's face darkened and she narrowed her eyes at Kimberli.

"Come on, Missy. You don't want to let us down like that skinny little skank, Sophia," Kimberli said.

"I thought we were going to get caught at her house! But we got rid of her quick enough," a girl named Lisa from the cheer squad said.

"Not quick enough. You guys had to post like all night to make it work," Kimberli said.

"What?" Missy said.

Kimberli's face went slack. Too much schnapps had made her lips loose.

"I can't believe it. Nate was right. He said it was all you guys," Missy said.

The other kids slinked out of the room leaving the five of them. Missy's cheeks flushed and her eyes glinted with truth.

"You lied about everything. You turned everyone against Sophia because you thought Nate liked her."

"No Missy. I didn't lie. She said all that stuff about you, I swear. We were just like having your back."

"My back? What? So you could paint a target on it for later? You've been using me to get to Nate."

"I don't need any help getting a guy."

"You are an awful person, Kimberli. The way you talk to Lindsey is embarrassing, for you that is. I'd pay money to watch her knock your block off." Missy's voice rose.

"Watch your step, Missy," Kimberli said.

"Or what?" Nate asked. "You'll get your minions to harass her like you did Sophia? Sophia is missing because of you and your bull. Don't you even care about that?"

"Nate, I-"

"Guys, keep it down. Somebody will hear us," Garrett said.

"Shut up, Garrett!" Kimberli shrieked.

A stack of mats in the darkened back corner toppled over with a thump, causing everyone to freeze.

"Yeah, Garrett. Shut up," Sophia hissed.

## CHAPTER TWENTY-FOUR

"Sophia? What are you doing?" Garrett asked.

She moved toward them in a ballet strut, long strides, toe to heel. She turned a pirouette and ended in a ballet position.

"Are, are you OK?" Garrett asked.

A slow, unhappy smile spread across her face. Tears rolled freely down her cheeks. Her hair hung in greasy, scraggly shards. She stood up straight and took a deep breath.

"OK? I'm better than OK," she said.

"Everyone has been looking for you," Nate said.

"Well, it looks like you found me. Garrett, thank your little sister for me. She let them in and they saved me."

"Let who in?" Garrett asked, terrified he already knew the answer.

"She's stoned, like her mom. I'm out of here," Kimberli said.

"Oh Kimberli. You'll want to stay for this," Sophia said.

She held up her hand and showed them she had one of the razors that had been left in her locker.

"I didn't do that, Sophia," Kimberli said, backing towards the exit.

Sophia's face turned malevolent. She held up her other hand in front of her face and placed the tip of the razor in the space between her pinky and ring finger.

"What are you doing? Sophia, stop it," Nate said.

"Stop it? I can't Nate. I'm a cutter and cutters cut. Isn't that what you wanted me to do, Kimberli?"

"No- I- no," Kimberli stammered.

Sophia laughed. There was no humor in it, only anguish.

"Nate, do something," Missy said.

"Missy," Sophia wept, "you were my friend, but you let that snake turn you against me. You need to see this too."

"Go ahead. Do what you came for," a voice came from behind them.

The kids instinctively grabbed on to each other. Three boys with pale skin and eyes as dark as a cave stood between them and the door.

"Do you see what you've made me do?" Sophia said.

Nate was torn which way to keep his focus. He tried to weigh who was the bigger threat, but his fear made his thoughts blur.

Sophia shrieked, and the decision was made for him. She pulled the razor down hard. They watched in horror as the blade moved down the valley of her fingers. He couldn't stop watching. Nate's feet were riveted to the spot, yet everything in him wanted to run.

Blood pooled on the floor beneath her, but she kept going. Beyond reasonable strength, she cut all the way through with a jerk. Her pinky finger fell with a sickening plop onto the floor.

Missy screamed.

"That's right! Scream!" Sophia lunged toward them and they scattered.

Kimberli was her target. In her panic Kimberli stumbled over some free weights and in an instant Sophia was on her. She was shrieking and slashing at Kimberli with that horrible blade.

Before any of them could react, the air split with the sound of the fire alarm. It was enough to snap

Nate back into reality. A mental picture of Danny Dietz firing his weapon despite his grave injury popped into his head. Move!

Nate jumped on Sophia's back. They flailed together. He was trying to grab her arms and pull her off Kimberli, but she was slick with blood and sweat. The razor sliced into the flesh on the back of his hand causing him to wail. Pulling his hand back, strands of Sophia's hair dangled in his clutched fist. Disgusted, he tried to shake the hair off, but the blood on his hand glued it in place.

He tried to get a better grip on Sophia's upper arms. Nate knew she was athletic, but he could feel her muscles ripple under his grip like snakes. Sophia growled and tried to bite him, spittle spraying from her open mouth.

Someone was banging on the outside of the door. The terrifying boys weren't standing in front of it anymore. They moved in unison toward the gruesome wrestling match. Lindsey ran headlong into the doors and shoved with all her might against them. They wouldn't budge. The banging continued, harder.

"Garrett! Help me!" Lindsey shouted.

The sprinkler system shot into action soaking the chaos. Garrett ran towards Lindsey. He lost traction on the wet floor, and his feet went out from under him. His head hit the concrete floor with a nauseating thud.

Lindsey whimpered in despair, "Garrett?"

He didn't get up.

Lindsey threw her whole body against the doors. The wet floor made it impossible to get traction. One of the doors flew open with shocking force, pulling Lindsey out of the room. Linda, on the other side, slammed into the hardwoods on her back. Linda stood up gingerly. Squinting, she tried to see through the veil of water that poured from the sprinkler system. The gym floor was as slippery as ice and she moved forward with care.

Lindsey clung to the door handle as if to avoid drowning. Inside the room, Linda saw Garrett lying motionless on the floor. Nate struggled with Sophia. Blood covered both of them. There was a heap on the floor underneath them. It took her a moment to register that it was a person. Missy cowered against the wall, hands covering her ears. Her mouth was open, but the crash of water and the blaring alarm drowned out her screams.

Linda's body moved before her brain could make sense of it. She rushed as quickly as she dared to Nate and Sophia. She grabbed Sophia's blood-soaked sleeve and with Nate's help they wrenched her arm up and behind her. That gave Nate enough leverage to do the same to her other arm. Together, the hauled her off the mass beneath her.

"Oh my God!" Nate exclaimed.

It was definitely a person. Blonde hair, a girl, maybe. The face was obliterated with blood and the nose appeared to be missing. The whitish jelly of fat visible in a large gash across the cheek area.

"Who?" Linda squeaked.

The sprinklers shut down, water dripping like tears off of every surface. Missy stopped screaming. Sophia sobbed, her head hanging down.

"Ms. Garza, help me," she whispered.

"What the hell is happening in here!" Linda shouted.

Nate's eyes were wide. Blood streaked his chest, arms, and face. Linda looked him over in an attempt to find the source of the blood. Her eyes traveled to the arm she had in her grasp. More confusion flooded her brain as she could see the space where Sophia's finger should be was bare.

The open door to the gym slammed shut with a sound that echoed dully in the room, leaving Lindsey on the other side. She slammed her fists against the door in a hopeless attempt to open it.

"It's too late for help."

Linda's attention turned toward the sound of a voice that was vaguely familiar. She felt all of her blood rush to her solar plexus; it was the boys with insect eyes.

"Jesus," she whispered.

The taller boy snapped his head in her direction. "No," he said.

"We're all going to die," Sophia said and her body shook with laughter.

Linda almost lost her grip on Sophia's arm. This couldn't really be happening, could it?

A small light appeared near the door and Linda's mind registered it as the door opening a crack, but she could clearly see the doors were shut. The light took the shape of a figure. Linda strained, trying to make out who or what it was. It couldn't be Lindsey, it was too tall. Her mind was trying to process what she was seeing, but her rationale rejected it. It looked like Inna.

# CHAPTER TWENTY-FIVE

"This ends now." Inna's voice, but Linda knew that was not possible. Inna was still in a coma at the hospital.

"Ms. Kerpin!" Nate exclaimed.

"No, it can't be," Linda said.

"Your permission to be here is revoked. You have to leave now," Inna said.

All of the Black Eyed Kids turned to her and in unison said, "We have permission to be here."

"Permission," Sophia muttered.

Sophia slumped to her knees, almost taking Nate and Linda with her. Her body convulsed with low rumbling laughter, a voice too deep to be her own. Terrified, Nate loosened his grip on her. He could hardly bear to touch her.

"It's too late, woman. We're here," she hissed. She slowly tilted her head to an unnatural angle to look up at Nate.

He dropped her arm and shrunk back. His worst imagining had come to life. She had black pits for eyes, as if a taxidermist had removed the natural ones and replaced them with glass. Sophia twisted direction and her other arm broke free from Linda's grasp. Linda's reflexes were dulled by shock and before she could defend herself, Sophia was on top of her. Her hands closed around Linda's throat and squeezed.

"This is what it feels like to have everything strangled out of you by the ones you trust the most. Now you know how she felt!" Sophia spit out the words into Linda's face.

Linda's blood turned to ice. How could they know? She saw Yvette's face swim into focus, she was crying. A despair so deep it physically hurt washed over Linda. Instinctively she clawed at Sophia's hands, disgusted when her fingers dug into the gaping wound of the missing finger. Just as quickly as Sophia had landed on her, Linda felt the weight of her lift. Inna towered over them.

Inna's feet were bare and she wore some type of loose fitting garments. Her hair was jumbled and wild. How could this be happening? Linda felt a dangerous shift in her mind. She knew that if she didn't get a grasp on reality she might lose her sanity for good.

The only thing she could think to do was scream, "Jesus, help us!" No sound came out of her damaged throat, but she shouted it with her mind as loudly as she could.

With unnatural strength, Inna grasped Sophia in a bear hug, holding her captive. Dangling from Sophia's claw-like grasp was Linda's little gold cross and chain. Sophia's face contorted and she looked like a wild animal trying to escape a hunter's trap. Linda coughed so hard it hurt her back. Her throat was an inferno of pain. She scrambled as far away from the scene as she could.

"Let go!" Inna shouted. "You can make them leave! Be released from the grasp! You can be free!"

Sophia went limp.

"Tell them, Sophia! Tell them!" Inna shouted.

Sophia started sobbing.

The three shark-eyed boys moved closer to Sophia and Inna.

Sensing he was no longer needed, Nate felt his way along the wall to where Missy crouched in a tight ball. Her knees were drawn up to her chest and she pressed her face into her thighs. She crushed her ears with her hands. He put his arms around her. Her entire body shook, or was that him? He couldn't be sure.

"Tell them!" Inna shouted.

"You can't be here," Sophia said weakly.

"We have permission," the tallest eyeless boy said. His face suddenly looked confused.

Sophia lifted her face and her eyes were back to normal. "Not anymore."

There was a flash of light. Nate covered his eyes. The doors burst open. Two firefighters and a heavy set security guard crashed into the room.

"Is everyone OK!" the security guard shouted.

Inna was gone. The monsters were gone. The bloody heap that was Kimberli moaned. Garrett was still motionless. Sophia collapsed into a pile onto the floor.

"No. No, we are not OK," Linda wheezed, tears rushing down her cheeks.

"We need paramedics in the gym, now!" shouted a firefighter.

"Are you hurt, kid? Is this blood yours! Can you walk?" the other firefighter asked Nate.

He nodded, "Most of it's not mine."

As Nate stood, he pulled Missy up with him. She was as limp as a dishrag and his injured hand made it difficult to grasp her. Her hands were still solidly clamped over her ears. She pressed her face to his chest. Nate half-walked half-carried her out of the gym into the crisp evening.

A bank of fog had rolled in sometime during the evening encasing the scene. Blue and red emergency lights were reflecting like beacons, letting everyone know something awful had happened here.

Mr. Greene was pacing in front of a fire engine. His phone pressed to the side of his face.

"Nate!"

His mom and dad stood on the sidewalk huddled with Lindsey. Mel was hugging her and they were under a rough blanket together. Mel dropped her side of the blanket and ran to him and Missy.

"Oh my God! Are you guys all right?" She hugged them both.

Paramedics reached them just as David and Lindsey did. Mel cried and clung to Missy. At the touch of her mom, Missy finally unburied her face and dropped her hands from her ears. She wept and clung to Mel. The stout security guard led Linda out of the school and sat her in the front seat of his car. Her pretty face was smeared with blood and drained of color.

He pushed his eyeglasses up on his bald head. "Are you injured?"

Linda looked at her hands. "No. Just my throat." Rings of blue and purple were visible on the delicate skin of her neck.

"I think this is yours."

In his outstretched hand, he held her gold cross. She took it from him and squeezed it.

"Good thing to have," he said.

Linda looked up at him, and he smiled gently. "Thank you." She read the name tag over her breast pocket. "Officer Baldwin. I think you might be right." A fresh wave of sobbing took her.

A parade of stretchers rolled through the door. Lindsey ran to the first one.

"Is he OK?"

"He's hit his head pretty hard. Stand back, Miss," the paramedic said.

The curly hair was plastered to his head with blood. His face was slack and pale.

"Please be OK, Garrett," she whispered.

She turned to the next stretcher. Blood was soaking through the thick bandages on Kimberli's face and head. Lindsey's stomach pinched. Sophia was on the final stretcher. Her face and hair were streaked with blood. Her arms and legs tightly secured to the stretcher. Her heavily bandaged hand looked like a club.

She locked eyes with Lindsey. "I'm so sorry. Tell everyone I'm sorry. I'm so sorry."

Lindsey stood speechless and watched the stretcher bump over the sidewalk.

Nate was at her side. "Wait a minute! You're missing Ms. Kerpin!"

"Sorry, kid. There's no one else in there," a paramedic said.

Nate's mouth hung open. "But she was in there! With those other kids or things!" He clenched his fists as he felt a wave of hysteria move over him.

"Nate, let the paramedics look at you," Lindsey said as she placed her hand lightly on his forearm. The touch brought calmness.

"Are you all right?" He looked at her. She was drenched and the knees of her jeans were torn away.

"Yes. No. I don't know. I have to go, Nate." Her voice cracked with emotion.

His arm felt cold where her hand had been. David came and led him gently to the back bumper of an ambulance.

Nate didn't pay attention to the paramedic that took his blood pressure and asked him questions. He watched Lindsey disappear into the same expensive black SUV that brought them home from Lydia's. It pulled out after one of the ambulances and chased it out of the parking lot and down the road, disappearing into the fog.

# CHAPTER TWENTY-SIX

In the following hours, Nate told his parents everything. Every weird and bizarre detail, he held nothing back. David shifted in his seat at regular intervals and crossed his arms over his chest. Mel shook her head knowingly; she had seen the Black Eyed Kids herself, after all. David perked up when the talk shifted to moving.

Almost two weeks had gone by and the early October day was bright. The sun felt warm on Nate's skin, but the breeze had the promise of winter in it. He felt constricted by his suit jacket and tried to adjust the shoulders for more room. David put his hand lightly on his back.

Missy and Mel did not join them. Neither of them were ready to face people. Nate suspected Missy wouldn't be ready for quite some time. She was different now, quieter, more introverted. Mel said it would pass, and she'd be back to her old self. He couldn't believe he missed her big mouth and big attitude, but he did.

Nate looked across the gathered circle to Ms. Garza. The simple black dress and sweater she wore swallowed her slight frame. Her face was drawn as if the experience aged her overnight. Tears glistened on her cheeks, and the sun glinted off a small gold cross on her chest. Bruises on her neck were barely visible. She sat next to Ms. Kerpin's husband in a metal folding chair in the place reserved for family.

Over the casket and the flowers, Nate could see Lindsey standing just behind Linda. Lydia wrapped her in a protective side hug. Lindsey's eyes never left the ground. In the days following what become known as, The Incident, she had taken down her website and dumped her cell phone. The darkness left nothing in their lives untouched or unchanged.

Nate shoved his hands in his pockets and fingered the little medal Lydia had given him.

When the service was over the crowd silently disbursed and Nate and David headed for their car.

"Nate? May I speak to you for a minute?" Linda approached them.

David nodded. "Sure. I'll wait by the car."

She forced a smile for him and brushed at a patch of white fur on her skirt.

"I got a dog. A big one. How are you doing?" she asked.

"I don't know. OK, I guess."

"Me too."

A gentle breeze jostled the golden leaves too stubborn to leave the oak branches that hung over them.

"I'm really sorry about Ms. Kerpin, but I'm not sure how this all happened. It feels like a bad dream. I'd think I was going crazy, but you saw it too," he said.

"I don't know what happened either, Nate. She couldn't have been there that night. Ben said she passed away right before all that happened. Yet she was."

"What am I supposed to do with this, Ms. Garza?"

"I don't know. I really don't. Some things are just beyond our understanding and ability to explain. I guess you just have to accept that."

"What if I can't? Then what?" he asked.

"I wish I knew. For now, let's just concentrate on healing, OK?"

"Do you think those boys, those things, are gone?"

She pinched her lips together. "I hope so." She reached up and fingered the cross around her neck. "If you ever need to talk, call me, all right?"

"I will."

"You should be proud of yourself, Nate. You were a real hero that night. Take care of yourself."

"You too, Ms. Garza." He turned from her and got in his dad's car.

Her words slammed around in his brain. He wasn't proud, and he didn't feel like a hero. He hadn't slept in his own bed since The Incident. In fact, the whole family slept in the family room, huddled together on couches and the floor. Fits of crying snuck up on him, causing him to hide out in the bathroom until they subsided. He jumped at every noise and compulsively peered out of every window he passed, looking for them. What would the Navy SEALs say about him now?

A car sat in their driveway.

"Who's here?" Nate asked.

"I think it's Mike," David said.

Mike Eubanks sat on the couch in their family room. The sun slanting in the window behind him darkened his features. Mel was wearing sweatpants and an oversized faded Denver Broncos t-shirt. The only sound was the soft purring of the refrigerator.

"I wanted to tell you in person," Mike said breaking the silence.

Mel looked to David and Nate. "Mike says Garrett is awake."

"Can I see him?" Nate asked.

"Soon. He's still not out of the woods yet," Mike said.

"That's great news," David said.

"Yeah."

The silence filled the air again.

"The last thing he remembers is going to the football game," Mike said.

"Maybe that's good," Mel said.

Nate couldn't help but agree it was a lucky break. That night was burned into his memory for the rest of his days. Nothing could erase it no matter how hard he tried.

"He's had other concussions from snowboarding. That might have made this one worse. My wife wants to sue the school district," Mike said.

David nodded his head.

"Do you know anything about Kimberli?" Mel asked.

"I spoke to her dad, I mean stepdad. He said her mom took her to Florida or something to stay at a hospital. She's going to need extensive surgery. He's taking his other daughter, Lindsey, away for a while."

A deep sting of loss shocked Nate. He hadn't spoken to her since The Incident. When he called her house phone her dad kept saying she wasn't home. He shouldn't have been surprised.

"What about Sophia?" Missy floated unnoticed into the room.

Mel jumped at the sound of her voice.

David said, "You don't need to worry about that."

"Do you know anything?" Mel asked, ignoring David.

Mike hesitated. "Matt, that's Kimberli's stepdad, spoke to the DA's office. She'll have a competency hearing sometime next week. The kids might get subpoenas in the mail. Matt made sure that they can submit testimony on video."

"Is she going to jail?" Missy asked.

Mike sighed. "I don't know. Matt's family wants her to. The DA said that Sophia's family is hoping the judge rules for hospitalization. In her present state of mind, they're afraid she wouldn't make it in juvie."

A surge of panic threatened to take Nate over. Testimony? What would he say? If he told all of it he'd end up next door to Sophia in the psych ward. If she ended up there, that was.

Nate saw her in his mind, sitting in a dingy cell on a steel frame bed with no mattress. Black-eyed boys taunted her from the other side of the bars. Reaching for her with hands with missing fingers, blood dripping on the floor. The sound of his name shook the vision away.

"Nate, Matt wants to talk to you when you feel up to it. He wants to thank you for what you did for Kimberli," Mike said.

Nate ran his finger over the raw scar on the back of his hand, "I didn't do anything."

"If you hadn't stopped Sophia, well, who knows what would have happened."

*Who knows*, Nate thought. *Absolutely no one.*

# CHAPTER TWENTY-SEVEN

She sat in the darkened room, a crisp white sheet that glowed in the dim room covered her from the waist down. The anesthetic was wearing off. She reached for the hand-held mirror on the bedside table and inspected the bulky gauze bandages wrapped around her chest. The bigger breasts weren't part of the work to repair the damage done by that psycho, Sophia, but her mother would agree to anything at this point.

Kimberli knew her stepdad had money, he was an executive at a bank after all, but she discovered that Mona came from old money, and plenty of it. She was sure Mona would drain every account to ensure that Kimberli recovered from her ordeal and Kimberli planned to take full advantage. Mona owed her that.

The money was kept quiet from her because Mona didn't want it to corrupt her. How her mother supported them in the time between husband number one left and husband number two came along never entered Kimberli's mind. But if it had, the question was now answered.

After Mona fessed up to the money she divulged an even bigger secret, the real reason that Kimberli's dad left them. Mona funded Kimberli's father's failed business attempts for years, but after she finally said no, he tried to drain a trust fund set up for Kimberli, so out he went. The information hadn't changed Kimberli's thoughts on the subject. It was still Mona's fault that her dad left, but now she knew there was plenty of money waiting for her when she turned twenty-five. She wouldn't need Mona after that.

Kimberli checked out her face in the mirror. She couldn't even tell where the tip of her nose had been slashed off, the reconstruction looked so natural. The scar from the gash that traveled from the corner of her mouth to mid-cheek was the only one noticeable now. At first, her face was a road map of slash marks, but the doctors at this private plastic surgery clinic were top-notch.

A flash of Sophia, *cutters cut.*

She pried her left eye open and recoiled. She wasn't sure she would ever get used to the empty cavity. Sophia had sliced the eyeball in half, right through her eyelid. The prosthetic eye was a perfect match for her good eye and she vowed never to let anyone see her without it. The scar on her lid could be easily covered with makeup, also something no one would see her without.

The familiar hot rush of anger flushed her face. That crazy little witch almost killed her, but here she still was. After all the surgeries she would be even better than before, and that psycho could rot in a cell. Kimberli wasn't just a survivor, but a thriver!

That was going to be the tagline of the book she was going to write about the whole mess.

The memories of that night were a little hazy but one thing truly confused her. Kimberli told the detectives that some boys she didn't recognize were there urging Sophia along. They assured her that there was no one else, Sophia acted on her own. It didn't matter. She would make sure that Sophia paid for what she had done and then some.

She read some of the news coverage on-line but quit after several users commented that Kimberli drove Sophia to it with the bullying. That's what was wrong with everyone, no one took responsibility for their actions, always looking for someone to blame. She was the victim here, and she planned to be at Sophia's hearing in person. The others would give video statements, but she wanted everyone to see that little bitch hadn't won. She'd walk into the hearing with her head held high, the brave and hauntingly beautiful survivor. Surely, she'd get her picture on the news. Maybe a casting director would see her and contact her, or a modeling agency would want her to be their number one girl. The possibilities were endless.

People ate up stories of those who overcame terrible tragedies. Look at that girl in India who got shot or something, for something Kimberli couldn't recall. Everyone loved her and she wasn't even pretty.

There was a slight knock on the door.

"Yes?"

The door cracked open and a young nurse wearing scrubs with cartoon dogs on them stood in the slim opening.

"How you doing?"

"Good. Can I get like a soda or something?"

"I'll see what the doc says."

The door slid shut.

She should have asked for more pain medication. She'd ask when the nurse came back with the soda. No reason to be uncomfortable. She shifted on the bed. Enough anesthesia from surgery remained in her system to drag her into a peaceful sleep.

She woke with a start, like the feeling of falling off the bed. Kimberli had no way of knowing how long she had been dozing, but the nurse obviously hadn't been back with her soda. A vague throb spread over her chest. She dug through the covers looking for the call button that was clipped to her pillow.

Someone knocked hard on the door.

*Finally.*

"About time! Come in!"

A young girl squirmed into the room. Her head was down and soft curls covered her face. Recognition slowly spread over Kimberli.

"Haley?" she breathed. "What are you doing here?"

The girl lifted her head and stared at Kimberli with eyes that were darker and emptier than her own vacant socket. The gloom of those eyes accused, condemned, and beckoned. Kimberli tried to scream, but fear squeezed her throat and a weak whistle is all that came out.

"Thank you for your permission," Haley said in a low voice not her own. "This won't take long."

The End

## About the Author

Joy Yehle is a Colorado-based writer. Growing up surrounded by otherworldly tales as told by her father and maternal grandmother, a love for the darker things in life solidly took root. One of her greatest pleasures is to pass on this love in a way that makes readers afraid to turn off the lights. When she is not terrorizing her audience, Joy can be found seeking out haunted places, old cemeteries, cryptids, U.F.Os and other strange things. If you don't find her there she is probably camping and hiking with her dear husband, their gaggle of kids, and a grey striped tabby cat.

For more scares, connect with her on her blog at
www.joyyehle.com
Facebook - www.facebook.com/joyyehle
Twitter - @JoyYehle
Instagram - joyyehle

Thank you for your purchase. Reviews are the life blood that keep the books you enjoy available. If you were entertained by this book, please consider leaving a review.